DANCER AND THE ICE BEAR
FURRY UNITED COALITION
BOOK IX

EVE LANGLAIS

Copyright Dancer and the Ice Bear © Eve Langlais

Cover Art by Dreams2Media © 2024

Produced in Canada

Published by Eve Langlais

http://www.EveLanglais.com

E-ISBN: 978 177 384 5180
Print ISBN: 978 177 384 5197

ALL RIGHTS RESERVED

This book is a work of fiction and the characters, events and dialogue found within the story are of the author's imagination and are not to be construed as real. Any resemblance to actual events or persons, either living or deceased, is completely coincidental.

No part of this book may be reproduced or shared in any form or by any means, electronic or mechanical, including but not limited to digital copying, file sharing, audio recording, email and printing without permission in writing from the author. Not to be be used for AI/artificial intelligence training.

PROLOGUE

> Only days before Christmas my true love
> gave to me... a kick in the nuts.

NANOOK LUMBERED BACK a day early from his fishing trip. He'd lucked out and caught a fat beluga whale and dropped most of it off at the butchers in Santa's Village. The remainder would feed his family well, and he could already hear the happy cooing of his girls. Roasted blubber chips, blubber soup, blubber pudding...

His stomach rumbled. It always did when he thought of food, which was often. He didn't get his barrel chest from eating berries like those puny black bears to the south.

As Nanook neared the jutting mountain of ice outside the village, where he'd carved out a home, he frowned to see the playpen sitting just outside the entrance. He spotted the girls trapped behind the chicken-wire coop, the only material that could withstand curious cubs. Odd, he didn't see his wife Anjij out there with them. Not exactly safe, given they'd had walrus humping their way inland recently.

Grawr. His cubs nosed the bars and made happy noises as they saw their Dada.

My precious girls. His mouth let go of the bag he'd been dragging as he crouched in front of the pen. He would have smiled at his cubs' excitement, only a bear's snout didn't curve. He could rub noses with them, though.

Where is Anjij? The children were too young to be left unattended for long outdoors. He shifted, his human skin pimpling at the cold air. He scooped his babies from their playpen and brought them into the ice-carved cave, kept warm with a small coal-burning pot belly stove in the center of the main room. He placed his children on the floor by their toy blocks—none of that wooden stuff that could splinter. He'd hand-carved these himself from narwhal horns. The perfect thing for a teething baby bear.

As his girls tumbled and fought over the same block, he grabbed his sealskin robe and slid on his slippers. Still no sign of Anjij. Had she taken ill?

He went deeper into his home, wondering at the strange noise he heard, a high-pitched choo-choo sound that reminded him of a whistling train.

The oddity grew louder as he reached the cave where he and his wife slept. He walked in to find Anjij doing the nasty with an elf. The male wouldn't have even stood knee-high on Nanook, and Anjij's thighs could have crushed him if she'd applied any pressure.

But she wasn't fighting the elf who pistoned his narrow hips as he plowed Anjij.

His wife.

Cheating on him.

With an elf?!!!

Nanook didn't think, just snapped. He shifted and roared.

Anjij screamed as she caught sight of him, and the elf came just as Nanook batted him aside, spraying the cave walls with peppermint-scented cum.

The little man recovered quickly and squeaked, "Calm down, fat ass."

He would not calm down. He'd eviscerate the stringy bastard.

Nanook prepared to charge, only Anjij planted herself in front of him and yelled, "Don't eat him."

How dare she defend the elf cuckolding him! Nanook bared his teeth.

She tossed back her glorious mane of hair and sniffed. "I'm not afraid of you."

He shifted to growl, "How could you? We're married."

"A mistake. I want a divorce."

He recoiled. Obviously, they couldn't stay together, but still it stung. "What of the girls?"

"Keep them. Motherhood isn't for me," she declared.

A shocking statement that left him speechless, but not her lover.

The squeaky toy chirped, "Anjij is much too young

and beautiful for a cave-bear life. We're going to travel the world."

"Don't you have a job in Santa's workshop?" Elves worked year-round for Santa, with only a week off between Christmas and New Year's.

"Life's too short to be a slave to a jolly fat bastard in a red suit."

Short? Elves lived for centuries. "You can't be serious," he exclaimed.

"I'm leaving with Jingles," Anjij stated. "We're in love."

"You can't be. You're in love with me."

Her lips tugged into a sneer. "Hardly. I married you to get out from under my dad's paw. I told you I didn't want to live in the North forever."

"We're polar bears. It's where we belong."

"Not me. I'm leaving."

"But it's almost Christmas." A word that soured in his mouth as Jingles dared to put on his pointed green cap with a bell on the end, which matched his red, white, and green striped outfit.

"Christmas is an excuse to enslave elves. I say down with the holiday!" Jingles exclaimed.

"Screw Christmas, and screw this place," Anjij added.

With that, Anjij departed with her lover, a lumbering polar bear with an elf riding on her back.

She didn't even say goodbye to the girls. Never once tried to contact them once she left.

Nanook tried to move past the betrayal, but each time he saw tinsel, or heard a Christmas song, or saw an elf, the pain—and rage—engulfed. Given everything about Santa's Village triggered him, he moved out of his ice cave and relocated. He raised the twins on his own, teaching them the way of the polar bears. Gave them his love, his knowledge, his loyalty. A single dad who would do anything for them... except celebrate Christmas, the one time of the year guaranteed to put him in a foul mood.

Bah hum-elf.

1

> Away in a snowbank,
> No sheet for her bed,
> The very drunken Dancer,
> Lay down her tined head…

A HUNGOVER DANCER woke and stretched, wondered why she was chilled, only to realize she'd passed out in a snowbank. Blame the pre-pre-pre-Christmas party, which had been quite the event. Candy cane shots, gingerbread rum cake, some brandied cherries. She'd partaken of it all, even as she knew she couldn't hold her liquor. No surprise she ended up wasted. She had a faint recollection of dancing on some tables—and throwing up on a potted poinsettia. At least she'd turned down the elf that propositioned her.

Utterly blasted, she didn't recall shifting into her reindeer shape or exiting the village. Thankfully, nothing ate her while she was passed out. Predators roamed outside Santa's Village, and some loved the taste of reindeer meat.

Dancer sat up and shook snow from her velvety antlers. Bad idea. Her head hurt, pounded like a child getting their first drum set under the tree. At her age, she should know better than to get sloshed, especially this close to Christmas. Santa expected all his reindeer to be in fit form, but in her defense, she'd been trying to mend her broken heart.

The bull she'd had her sights set on was engaged to another. It should be noted Rudolph never showed her the slightest interest, and yet she'd been hopeful that—as she was the only other reindeer misfit—they'd be naturally drawn to each other. Him with his glowing red nose, her with the horny nubs that didn't disappear when she shifted. Her deformity meant she couldn't date outside of, or even leave, the North Pole because she couldn't be seen in public—unless she wanted to end up with her head mounted on someone's wall or as a lab specimen dissected by curious humans.

Her inability to leave the North Pole shattered her dream of one day becoming a FUC agent and fighting crime. Some would say she should be happy she got to work for the jolliest man on Earth, but those people obviously had never worked for the big man. Santa trained them hard, had to since he wouldn't lay off the jelly donuts. They'd had to reinforce the sled for the second time in as many years.

Thinking of her boss made her squint at the dark sky, the usual for this time of the year in the North Pole. They wouldn't see sunlight again until March.

According to the position of stars, morning fast approached, and if she didn't get moving, she'd be late for sleigh training. Not a good idea, as it would ruin her bid to lead the team this year. Not that she stood a chance. Rudolph had the big guy wrapped around his ruby-red nose.

Dancer pushed herself up from the snow, swaying on her wobbly legs. Maybe she should send a message she couldn't make training because she was sick. Sick with the candy cane flu.

A scream from inside the village made the nutcrackers in her head clack their jaws harder. Ow. Some people had zero consideration for the hungover.

"Run for your lives!" an elf yelled, his high-pitched voice carrying and adding to the pounding discomfort.

Probably a Yeti incursion. They liked to raid around Christmas, knowing the elves would be baking their favorite treat—fruit cake. The QUEEFS—Quick Uber Elite Elf Fighting Squad—would handle it. The combat-trained elves were the village defence against predators. Dancer had applied when her dream of being a FUC agent fell through, but not being an elf, she got rejected immediately.

Totally unfair.

Dancer took a moment to stretch her stiff limbs. At least she'd shifted before collapsing in the snowbank. Nothing worse than waking up with frostbite, especially given the remedy tasted so foul. Whoever came up with the idea of mixing cinnamon with bourbon, crème de menthe, and turkey broth should have their taste buds checked.

As she rose to her wobbly hoofs, more yelling occurred. The QUEEFS must have mustered to repel the Yeti.

As she went to totter around the mound of snow—sidestepping a pile of puke with chunks of cherries—a puffin came waddling past.

She bleated a querying note at his panic.

The puffin, known as Joe, paused, and his eyes widened at the sight of her.

"Run!" squeaked her friend, who could speak in his bird shape.

She huffed. As if she'd flee. It was just a Yeti. The QUEEFS would toss it some fruitcakes until it stopped smashing the gingerbread houses. Not exactly the best building material, but the elves preferred it over igloos.

"It's not a Yeti," Joe huffed, understanding her disdain. "The village is being attacked by Krampus."

She uttered a scoffing snort.

"I swear it's true. Someone calling themselves Krampus has arrived with an army. Santa's workshop is under siege."

Her muzzle dropped open in shock.

"He's got wolverines and walrus rounding up everyone. Flee while you can."

Flee? No way. This was her chance to fight. Dancer suddenly had visions of grandeur. If she saved Christmas, Santa would be so thankful he'd let her lead the sleigh instead of Rudolph.

Joe scurried off as something exploded in the village and sent up a cloud of multicolored smoke. The damage to the paint factory would slow down production in the New Year. Good thing the elves had already finished this year's batch of toys.

Despite her pounding head, she had to act, even as she didn't know what she could do. She'd never trained to fight. Then again, perhaps Joe misunderstood the situation. Puffins weren't known for their intelligence. A peek at the situation seemed called for.

A quick trot brought her around the snowbank and in sight of the village.

A village under attack.

Elves ran to and fro, chased by wolverines who appeared to be herding them in the direction of Gingerbread Hall. Walrus stood guard at the village entrance, kind of a misnomer since there was no wall or fence around the place.

While the place appeared overrun, the QUEEFS were trying their best to repel. Armed with candy cane shooters, hot cocoa throwers, and licorice whips, they went after the invaders. However, a forty-pound elf was no match for a ridiculously heavy walrus.

The red and white striped missiles bounced off the hide of the big male that humped its way toward the squad, which splintered and bolted in different directions.

As she watched, another explosion rocked the snow underfoot, and a river of hot taffy began rolling through the icy lanes, coating everything in its path, from elf to walrus. It proved especially painful to listen to Freezo the Snowman scream, "I'm melting."

It occurred to Dancer that she alone would not be enough to turn the tide. Walrus outweighed her and could be nasty with those goring tusks. Wolverines loved to tear out tendons to topple the four-legged. Saving the village would require help beyond that which the QUEEFS could provide, but the nearest FUC outpost was in Greenland, which meant crossing the Arctic Sea. She could swim, but she'd freeze, drown, or get eaten before she managed to traverse the five hundred-plus miles.

It would have been an easy trip if she could fly, only she couldn't soar without Santa's dust, which he kept locked away in a vault along with his bible of Good and Naughty Children.

However, she knew where to find a hidden stash. Her good friend Comet had managed to filch some so she could visit her boyfriend in Alert, Nunavut.

Dancer retreated from the village and trotted to the training field where Santa had an obstacle course set up for them to run their paces. Chimneys for them to leap over. Narrow roofs that required precise landing lest the sleigh fall off. Steep sloping tile. Asphalt surface. Woven grass. Every kind of roof dotted the field, as Santa took their training seriously.

The special dust had been tucked inside a chimney, and as Dancer pulled the baggie out with her teeth, she heard a grunt. A glance behind showed a walrus humping in her direction.

Jumping hollyberries, she had to speed up. Dancer tugged at the drawstring with her teeth, loosening it enough to see there weren't many precious sprinkles left.

DANCER AND THE ICE BEAR

A loud whistle by the walrus brought some wolverines yipping.

Time to go. She upended the bag, and dust dumped out, landing on the hard ice. Dancer bent her head and sniffed the powder, feeling it tickle as it went up her nose. She would have liked to have snorted more, but those wily polar devils were coming at her fast.

Hopefully she'd inhaled enough. She began to run, her long legs stretching, her adrenaline sluggishly waking and erasing the last remnants of her hangover.

She didn't have a proper runway to get up to speed. However, she did have motivation, as the racing wolverines got closer, slavering with excitement.

On Dancer and Dancer and Dancer and Dancer. She encouraged herself using Santa's chant, wondering if any of her reindeer friends survived the attack. She almost stumbled at the thought she might be the only one left.

A chimney in her way led to her making a mighty leap. For a second, she remained aloft, but the powder hadn't fully taken effect. She needed her blood coursing, moving the dust through her body. She huffed hotly as she strained, moving her legs rapidly.

Snap. The jaws that snapped much too close to her hindquarters startled her into jumping again, her legs still pedaling. This time she didn't sink back down. She went up.

And up.

Only as she realized she flew did she glance down to see the wolverines converging under her, muzzles upturned in anticipation.

Not today, mongrels.

Dancer ran on air, heading for the Arctic Sea, racing as fast as she could, knowing the power would run out and she needed to reach land before that happened. She used the stars to guide her route, something she'd been taught but never had to do before. It was eerie flying by herself. Usually, she only ever took the skies with the team. But if Comet could do it to get laid, then so could she!

She might have made it to Greenland had a storm not suddenly developed. Dark clouds, heavy snow, whipping winds. She fought against the buffeting tempest, disoriented, tired, but determined.

Bad weather wasn't new. She'd flown through worse. Only, she usually had Santa and Rudolph to guide her.

When the dust began to fail, she found herself losing altitude, sinking, sinking. The only reason she didn't panic? The dark churning sea had changed to white, meaning she'd reached solid ground. She kept descending, readying to land. The storm chose to kick up a notch, rendering visibility to nil, which was how she ended up slamming into a mountain.

2

'Twas the week before Christmas and all
   through the cave
The children were storm-bound but didn't
   misbehave.
No stockings were hung, because they
   were unaware,
Blame their Dada, a grumpy ice bear.

The cubs were wearing their white
   fluffy fur,
Adorable and cuddly, anyone would
   concur.
Dada snored soundly with the twins in
   his lap,
Only they couldn't settle down for an
   afternoon nap.

When outside their home there arose a big
   thump,

> The girls sprang from his lap to see what
> had bumped.
> Away to the door they scurried and
> fought,
> Siku flipped open the curtain, and her jaw
> dropped.
>
> A storm had dumped a new foot of snow,
> And a chilly wind took that moment to
> blow.
> Still what to their wondering eyes should
> appear,
> A naked lady with antlers—a reindeer!

NANOOK HEARD the excited shrieks and grumbled. Why, oh why, wouldn't his darling hellions nap anymore? There used to be a time when they'd all snuggle in a furry big pile, having the grandest slumbers. However, his daughters, having recently turned five, made it clear those days were done.

He rolled from his comfy chair to the floor on his four paws and gave a quick glance around. He could hear their excited chatter but didn't see them inside the cave. Those precocious brats had gone outside into the nasty storm.

Before he could exit and give them a stern scolding, and see what had their fur in a fluff, they entered huffing and chuffing. Pure white and cuddly, their coats laced in snow, seeing their blatant disregard for his rules led him to shift and bellow, "What were you doing outside without me?" While he encouraged independence, he did require they remain within his sights, given the predators that would gladly take down a still-learning cub.

Siku shifted and clapped her hands as she squealed. "Dada! We found something."

"Found what?"

The reply came from Sesi, who also transformed. "A woman with horns."

He blinked, mostly because the statement made no sense. "Do you mean a caribou?" Herds of them inhabited Ellesmere Island.

"Yes and no. You have to help her. She was too heavy for us to lift." Siku pointed to the doorway with its weighted leather flap to keep out most of the snow and cold drafts.

Obviously, there was a communication issue. While his girls were highly intelligent, their young age made them perceive the world differently than an adult. Still, their claim bore checking out.

"You stay here while I go have a look."

He swapped back into his bear rather than get dressed. Maybe he could finish that nap before dinner.

Out into the storm he lumbered, the whipping snow reducing visibility and clinging to his fur, not that it bothered him. They didn't call his kind ice bears for nothing.

He didn't have to go far to find what had his daughters in a tizzy. He immediately spotted the woman lying in a heap in the snow.

A nude female to be exact, smelling of caribou, with antler nubs peeking from her hair.

He blinked, but the horns remained. Well damn. His daughters weren't confused after all. But he had a dilemma. What to do with her? Leaving her outside, she'd die for sure. Bringing her inside meant dealing with a stranger. He didn't like outsiders, or people in general.

In this scenario, he didn't have a choice. He'd warm her up and set her on her way. He grabbed the female and heaved her over his shoulder. He brought her inside and dumped her naked butt on the wolf skin rug. She flopped onto her back, which meant noticing, despite her frigid pallor, the stranger had an attractive countenance and a fine form.

While not a gentlebear, he glanced away.

Siku clapped her hands. "She's pretty. Can we keep her?"

"Yes, Dada, can we?" Sesi squealed.

He shifted and grabbed his robe before muttering, "No, we cannot keep her. She's not a pet."

"I know that," Siku huffed, rolling her eyes. Where had she learned that? Probably her cousins whom they'd visited recently when they went to get supplies.

"She can be our mommy," Sesi declared. She and her twin had been bugging him of late about how they didn't have one. Apparently, they'd reached an age where they noticed such things. When they asked where their mother went, rather than say *off sucking an elf's dick*, he'd muttered, *She died*. Seemed kinder than explaining the slag abandoned them without a second thought.

"You can't just decide a random stranger is going to

be your mother," he pointed out, tossing a blanket over the stranger. His logic didn't deter his stubborn girls.

"Yes, we can," Siku insisted. "Rory got a new daddy. Rory says his mommy found him when she went to Alert for supplies." Patty never met a man she didn't want to bring home, although the most recent one had lasted longer than most at six months.

"How come you never brought home a mommy when you went to Alert?" added Sesi. Alert was the nearest town, if you could call a place with less than two hundred people a town. Ellesmere Island being remote with harsh seasons didn't exactly boast a huge population. A few hundred people at most.

"Because we don't need a mother. You have me, the best father ever."

The girls eyed each other and used that secret twin connection they'd been born with to say in synchronization, "We want one."

"This one," Siku emphasized.

"The answer is no. It's not up to the kids to choose a mommy."

"Who chooses then?" Sesi cocked her head as she asked.

"Is there a store to find a mommy?" his other innocent daughter asked.

Was he really going to have to tell them about the bears and the bees? "You can't buy a mommy, or a daddy for that matter." Then, because they were opening his mouths to bombard him, he added, "What usually happens is a man and a woman will meet, and if they really like each other, they might decide to live together and be a family."

"How can you meet someone when you don't go anywhere?" Siku pointed out.

"And you hate everyone," Sesi stated.

His girls knew him all too well, and they raised valid points, which he didn't want to address, so he diverted their reasoning. "Has it occurred to you that maybe this woman doesn't want to be a mommy?"

Again, the twins shared a secret look before saying, "Why wouldn't she want us?"

Siku's lower lip jutted. "Are you saying we're not cute?"

"Are we not perfect?" Sesi's eyes brimmed.

"Of course, you're cute." And excellent at using it to their advantage. "And perfect." Perfectly capable of driving him up an iceberg.

"Then she will want to be our mommy and tuck us in and read us stories—"

"And bake cookies!" Sesi declared, interrupting her sister.

Nanook held in a sigh. He'd been doing that more and more often of late. It began when his cubs learned to speak and had been snowballing as their bright little minds grasped more than they should.

Who knew what they'd start demanding once they started school? They'd turned five, and while they didn't have to attend kindergarten by law at that age, he knew they'd have to go to school eventually, which meant moving from his very remote cave to a place with people.

He disliked most people, but he loved his daughters, hence why they'd be relocating in the spring so they could start school in the fall. Not in Santa's Village, though, even if they had an excellent scholastic program. He still couldn't see or hear about anything Christmas without getting into a snarling rage.

"Tell you what. Once we move to the cape, I will hire a nanny who can bake and read stories." A good compromise in his mind.

"A nanny is not a mommy," Sesi stubbornly insisted.

"Close enough. Now enough of that kind of talk. I think she's waking."

Indeed, the woman stirred, rustling the fur blanket covering her lush frame.

A body he surprisingly admired. How long since he'd paid any attention to the opposite sex? He blamed his daughters' big idea for his ogling. Making this random stranger their mommy, indeed. Never again. He'd sworn off relationships after the fiasco with Anjij.

The stranger opened her eyes, blinked at him, and murmured, "Please don't eat me, Mr. Bear." Her sense of smell must be working.

Siku giggled. "Dada doesn't eat people. His favorite food is whales."

"Which are blech." Siku stuck out her tongue. "Burgers are better."

"Er, what?" The woman blinked and sat up, holding the blanket to her chest as she glanced around. "Where am I?"

"In our house," Sesi chirped.

"And your house is where, exactly?" Asked as she

stood. The stranger put a hand to her head and swayed on her feet. "Oh, peppermint sticks. I must have crashed hard."

"Were you driving a snowmobile?" Siku asked. "Uncle Arnie broke his. Aunt Kira said he crashed it 'cause he's a dumb bear who rides too fast."

"No, no snowmobile. I was flying," the woman murmured.

"You're a bird?" Sesi's nose wrinkled, and Nanook understood her confusion. The woman's scent was the distinct one of a caribou… but caribou didn't fly. It hit him then. *Oh, frozen shitsicle.*

"You're a reindeer!" Which, for the confused, was the European name for caribou. Why the difference, he couldn't have said.

"I am. And you're a polar bear. Now that we've gotten that out of the way—"

"You're one of *them*," Nanook harrumphed, glaring at her.

"Excuse me?"

"One of the reindeer on *his* team," he growled, avoiding the S word.

"I am." Her chin lifted. "Dancer Lightfoot, second lead. And you are?"

"Not interested in dealing with you. Buh-bye." He stood by the door and gave a scooting gesture.

She pursed her lips. "It's still storming outside."

"And?"

"While I'd love to accommodate your request, it would be foolish of me since I can't get my bearings until it stops."

A valid point. "Fine, you can stay until it dies down, but then I want you gone."

"Goodness. Someone is a Grinch," Dancer huffed.

"What's a Grinch?" asked Sesi.

"Someone who hates Santa," the woman replied.

"What's a Santa?" was Siku's next question.

"Wait, how do you not know who Santa is?" Dancer sounded shocked.

Nanook had to act fast. "Girls, if you don't mind, I'd like a private chat with our guest."

"But, Dada, we found her," whined Sesi.

"Finders-keepers, remember?" Siku reminded.

"That doesn't apply to people," he snapped as he grabbed Dancer by the arm and dragged her from the main living area to his bedroom. Before he could explain she needed to keep her Santa nonsense to herself, Dancer exclaimed, "This is the nicest cave I've ever seen. It's so big. How many rooms?"

"Five. Now about—"

"Five? It's a veritable mansion. Did you carve it out of the mountain yourself?"

"Parts of it, yes. Now—"

"This is very impressive." She dragged her fingers over the smooth wall, chiseled in his spare time.

The compliment puffed his chest but did nothing for his attitude. "Forget about my house. It isn't important. You are not to mention Santa or anything Christmas to the girls."

"Why ever not?"

"Because Christmas is banned in my home."

"Banned?" She ogled him. "Isn't that unfair to your daughters?"

She zeroed in on the guilt he kept stuffing down—deep down. Not everyone celebrated that dreaded holiday. His girls were doing just fine. "They can't miss what they don't know."

"But what about their presents? I'll bet they're on Santa's good list. You're depriving them of—"

"Nothing. They have everything they could need. A roof over their head. Food for their bellies. Books to read."

"What about toys?"

"They have some, but then again, who needs fabricated items when there's a world outside to explore?"

"Glad you're not my dad," she muttered.

So was he because his body's reaction to the very attractive reindeer would have been wildly inappropriate.

"Why are you out in a storm, anyhow? Shouldn't you be at the village getting ready for the big day?"

Her lips turned down. "Usually, yes. However, we've been invaded. Krampus has taken over the village and appears to have captured everyone, including Santa."

"Krampus isn't real."

"That's what I said, but Joe—"

"Who's Joe?" he interrupted to ask, wondering at the fact his fists clenched.

"A puffin. He saw it go down. Apparently, this person who ambushed the village and took everyone hostage is calling themselves Krampus. I was on my way to fetch some help to free everyone when the storm hit."

"Get help from where? There's nothing this far north on Ellesmere Island other than FARTZ." The name for the research camp, which stood for Furry Arctic Research Team of Zoologists.

"Ellesmere Island!" Her voice squeaked. "I was aiming for the FUC outpost in Greenland."

He snorted. "Yeah, not even close. Storm must have turned you around."

"Oh, that's not good," she muttered. "I ran out of flying dust. How will I get to Greenland now?"

"You won't."

Her lips pinched. "That's not helpful."

"But it is honest."

"Surely there's a way from here to there."

"Alert's the place you would go to for transport off the island, but this time of year, those flights are for military personnel only."

Her brow creased. "Is there no other way?"

"There's Charlie. He's got a chopper, but he doesn't come cheap." And she obviously had nothing to her name, not even clothes.

"Can I borrow your satellite phone?"

"Don't have one."

"You can't be serious." She stared at him in shock.

"Said by the lady who doesn't have one either."

"I left it in my cabin when I went to the party last night."

"Must have been quite the party if no one noticed this Krampus attacking." Santa had defenses to protect the village from outside forces. Someone must have fallen asleep on the job.

"I'm not sure how they got close with no one noticing. I woke up while the attack was in progress. I might have had too much to drink and passed out in a snowbank," she muttered ruefully.

He couldn't mock her because he'd had that happen a time or two or three. "Maybe someone else made it to Greenland or managed to call FUC and reinforcements are on their way."

"Maybe." A doubtful reply.

"Once the storm lets up, you can head into FARTZ—"

"Why would I walk into a stink?"

"FARTZ is a scientific settlement of shifters. Think of it as a very mini town. Folks there will have a phone you can use. Someone might even be willing to take you to Alert or help you out with Charlie."

"I guess I don't have a choice." She glanced down at her state of undress. "I realize I'm imposing. However, do you have anything other than a blanket for me to wear?"

While his wardrobe proved limited—he tended to spend mostly on his daughters—he did manage to loan her a shirt that hung on her like a dress and some flannel pants that she had to knot at the waist. Add in socks for her bare feet and she was covered in the ugliest, baggiest outfit, yet remained attractive.

"Thank you..." She paused. "I don't think you've told me your name."

"Nanook. And the girls are Sesi and Siku."

"You're raising them by yourself?" Kind of obvious, given the bedroom held nothing feminine, not even a scent.

"Yeah." He didn't add anything more.

"Dada!" The demanding bellow could have been either cub.

"Excuse me while I tend to my daughters." Nanook exited his room to see the girls standing side by side with matching expressions that screamed twin trouble.

"What is it?" he asked, already dreading the reply.

"Dancer is lost," Siku began.

"Wait, were you eavesdropping?" he interrupted with suspicion.

"No. You're just loud. We heard her. She needs help," Sesi stated.

"And?" he asked with a scowl.

"We've decided you have to help Dancer." A dual announcement.

He arched a brow. "You have?"

"Yes. She needs a hero, and you're a hero, so you have to help her," Sesi explained as if he were an idiot.

"I'm not a hero." More an ornery man.

"Yes, you are," Sesi insisted.

Siku nodded. "You save us all the time."

He did because his cubs loved to explore and find trouble. "That's being a father, not heroism."

"It's okay, girls. While I'm sure your dad is great and all, I need someone with actual fighting experience. I don't suppose this FARTZ place has any QUEEFS?" Dancer queried.

He startled at the word until he remembered what it

stood for. "No elves live on the island." He'd have eaten them if they tried.

"And no FUC agents either, you said. Surprising."

"Dada is a FUC," Sesi announced.

"Was FUCDD," he corrected. "Special ops branch but I retired a long time ago." FUCDD being the Furry United Coalition Department of Defense. Their military branch.

"I wanted to join, but these"—she indicated her horns—"made it so I couldn't leave the village."

"They're permanent?"

Dancer nodded. "I'm a bit of a freak. When I was young, the other reindeer used to laugh and call me names. But I showed them. I trained hard and worked my way up the ranks until I became my boss's number two."

He appreciated the fact she avoided using *his* name. Not that he had a problem with Santa. The big guy had been great to work for.

"What's your job?" Sesi inquired.

A hesitating Dancer glanced at him before murmuring, "Transport logistics."

He snorted and then coughed to hide his amusement. "Girls, Dancer is probably hungry and thirsty. Why don't you make her a snack?"

"Yes, Dada," they chimed in synchronization and scurried off to the area set up as a kitchen. A misnomer since it had no fridge, cupboards, or even a stove, unless the hearth counted. He used the space to store their dry food supplies, along with his dishes.

With the kids out of earshot, his curiosity had him

asking, "When you say this Krampus took everyone hostage, how? Were they that fearsome? Did they have powers like Santa?" The big guy could do things that defied explanation. It wasn't a stretch that someone calling themselves Krampus might as well.

"I don't know much since I fled before I could be captured. What I do know was the village was overrun by walrus and wolverines. So many of them. Blew right through the QUEEFS."

"I'm surprised those two species are working together."

"That's not the only surprise. I didn't think anything could defeat Santa."

"Are you sure he was captured? You said you left right away. For all you know, the big guy mounted a counteroffensive."

Her lips pursed. "You raise a good point. In my haste to escape, I assumed the worst."

"Meaning you might be panicking for nothing."

"Maybe. You really don't have a phone?"

"I don't. Then people might try and talk to me." He grimaced.

"Not the social type, eh?"

"Nope."

"Then I guess I really need to be thankful you've let me stay here out of the storm."

Before he could reply, his daughters returned with their idea of a snack.

Hot mug of milk—made from the powdered stuff—and puffed blubber. Essentially fat slow cooked until it got crispy.

"Whale crunchies and milk!" Sesi chirped.

Dancer took the offering, and her lips quirked. "My favorite. Thank you, girls. While getting lost in a storm wasn't on my holiday bingo card, I am so glad I bumped into your mountain."

He glared at her use of the word holiday. She didn't seem to notice.

"What's bingo?" Sesi asked.

"A game," Dancer replied. "A fun one where you get to scream if you win."

Sesi's eyes lit up. "Oooh. Can you show us?"

"Might as well since that storm isn't letting up anytime soon. I'll need a few things though."

And that was how Nanook went from a nice nap to listening to his daughters holler as they yelled Bingo.

3

> Dashing through the storm,
> without a freakn' sleigh.
> Trying to save Santa,
> but crashed along the way.

OF ALL THE BAD LUCK. How could Dancer have ended up so off course? And smashing into a mountain? A good thing the other reindeer weren't there to see or she'd have been mocked for sure. She could practically hear the snarky Vixen say, *Rudolph wouldn't have gotten lost.*

Things to be thankful for? At least she'd not frozen to death. Even better, she had food and shelter and company, of sorts. A certain grouchy ice bear made it clear he wanted her gone; however, his daughters seemed delighted by her presence.

A good thing Sesi and Siku—which were Inuit for Snow and Ice—had insisted on giving her shelter, even as their dad had grumbled and scowled. Jerk. And not just because of his attitude. Who didn't tell his kids about Santa?!

Given Dancer couldn't go anywhere in the blizzard, she kept herself distracted by teaching the adorable girls the joy of Bingo. The twins took after their Dada, their hair just as white as his, their eyes an icy blue. Talkative and outgoing, the twins kept a steady chatter going, unlike their recalcitrant father.

How did such a grumpy bear create such happy daughters? She wondered even more about his hatred of Christmas. Who banned it from their home and denied their children the joy of believing in the jolly fat man who gifted presents around the world?

"Where do you live?" Sesi asked as they progressed from Bingo to a puzzle of Canada that had images of the animal species in each province and territory.

At Father Bear's warning glare, she kept it vague. "I have a cabin in the North Pole."

"What's transport logistics?" Siku's query.

"I help to bring stuff to places." Technically accurate.

"Do you have kids?" The interrogation continued.

"No."

"Do you want some?" Siku bluntly inquired.

"Eventually."

"Girls," Nanook grumbled, but his daughters turned beaming smiles on him and cooed, "Yes, Dada dearest?"

"Stop pestering our visitor. Get ready for dinner." As they scooted off to wash their hands, she commented, "Cute kids."

"I'm aware. Although I could do without the million questions."

"They're curious." She was too. Why live out here all alone?

She followed him to the kitchen cave where he began ladling his fragrant stew. "Have you lived here long?"

"Long enough."

The girls returned and fought over who would sit beside Dancer. They both did, and Dada Bear stood, since there were only three stools.

"Do you like seal soup?" Sesi asked, slurping a spoonful.

"Yes."

"What's your favorite food?" Siku's turn.

"Right now, your dad's stew. This is delicious." While many reindeer stuck to an herbivore diet, Dancer leaned toward an omnivore palate.

"Dessert?" The questions kept coming.

"Apple pie with cinnamon crumble on top."

"Ooh, Aunt Kira made an apple pie once. It was yummy," Sesi exclaimed.

"I like chocolate," the other twin confided.

After dinner, they went back to their puzzle until Dada Bear announced, "Time for bed."

"Do we have to?" the pair whined.

"Yes." He crossed his arms.

The twins turned to Dancer. "Will you read us a story?"

Flattered, she smiled. "Of course."

The girls took her each by a hand and led her to their room, a cave bigger than their father's, with water trickling down the back wall into a basin that didn't overflow. Their bed was girly to the extreme. Covered in a pink comforter, with all kinds of pillows and stuffies. Apparently, Nanook didn't mind toys, just Christmas.

Dancer was told to sit between them as she read, a story about a princess who taught a dragon a lesson. The twins leaned against her and exclaimed each time she changed her voice to match a character. When she finished and did the awkward crawl out, their arms lifted as they pleaded, "Tuck us in."

As Dancer leaned over to draw the covers over them and place a soft kiss on their foreheads, Nanook entered and grumbled, "Not happening, my darling hellions."

What wasn't happening?

The twins grinned and murmured, "We'll see about that."

Must be some kind of family joke.

Dancer left and headed for the main living area as their father said goodnight. The storm still blew hard outside, meaning she'd be stuck here until it cleared.

Nanook joined her but appeared intent on ignoring Dancer. As if she'd allow that.

"Your girls are adorable."

"I'm aware."

"Their mother..." She hesitated to ask but also didn't want or need a wife to suddenly find Dancer alone with her husband and freak out.

"Isn't in the picture."

"Oh. I'm sorry to hear that."

"Don't be. She made her choice."

By his tone, he didn't approve, and it still bothered. She changed the subject.

"I know you said no phone, but surely you have a way of contacting people in case of emergency?"

"No."

"Isn't that dangerous considering you have two young kids?"

"None of your business." The frown aimed in her direction didn't have the expected effect. She'd been subject to Santa's stern glare, and he was much scarier.

"What if something happened to you?" she insisted.

"Nothing has."

"But it could."

"I'm a polar bear. Ain't much that can harm me," his dry reply.

"Hunters with long rifles can. Wolves. Walrus."

"Wolves know better than to come inside my territory. As for the fat wallies... I'd like to see them try." He bared his teeth.

Must be nice to have such confidence. A reindeer had ten times the threats.

A glance around showed objects that had to have been purchased, leading her to say, "How do you trade for supplies? Do you have to drag them back a piece at a time?"

"I have a snowmobile with a sled."

"And you didn't mention this before because...?"

"Because I'm not loaning a stranger my only motorized means of transportation," his retort.

"Fair enough, but you could drive me to civilization."

"I could."

"But won't," she guessed.

"Don't need nothing."

"Surely you care a little bit about the fact Santa and all his workers have been taken hostage?" She tried to rouse his sense of compassion.

And failed.

"Not really."

"What of the children who will be disappointed Christmas morning?"

"What part of I hate Christmas don't you grasp?" he snapped.

"Why?"

"None of your business."

As he studiously ignored her to mend a hole in a sock, she pursed her lips. Something kept nagging her brain. A little worm squirming, insisting she missed something. Nanook. His name seemed familiar and not just because it meant bear in Inuit.

It hit her suddenly. A rumor that floated around a few years ago. A scandal that rocked the elves in the village but the reindeer didn't pay much mind to.

She dumbly blurted out, "Are you the Nanook whose wife ran off with one of Santa's elves?"

His head whipped up so fast she almost got whiplash for him. "I'm not discussing this."

"So it was you." She paused. "I'm sorry. That must have been devastating."

"What part of not discussing it do you not get?" He rose and towered over her, looking grim and angry.

"If it helps, what she did was wrong. Especially

considering you have kids. It probably doesn't help you have to see her each time she visits with them."

"She doesn't visit." A blunt admission.

It dropped her jaw. "What? But she's their mother."

"Not in her mind." He moved away from Dancer.

It took her a moment to process. A mother who'd cheated then left and abandoned her children. It roused her ire, and she huffed, "Well, she's permanently on the naughty list."

He snorted. "As if she cares. We all know Santa only gifts the young believers."

True. Santa specialized in toys for children. The expansion that would be required to reward adults who behaved well all year would be... probably not be that bad given many had difficulty staying out of trouble.

"I'm sorry. That must have been rough. In good news, your daughters seem very happy and healthy."

"They are."

"But don't they need friends?" She couldn't stop putting her hoof in her mouth.

To her surprise, he softly admitted, "They do, which is why we'll be moving to the FARTZ encampment by spring so they can attend school in the fall."

"Doesn't sound you're like enamored of the idea."

"Don't like people."

Not exactly a surprise. "Surely you don't hate everyone. I mean, granted, there are some folks that are real rabbit turds, but not everyone is the same."

"Must you talk incessantly?" He sighed.

"Well, you don't have internet or cable, and I'm

pretty sure you don't want to play Bingo anymore. Guess you're my only hope for entertainment."

At her claim, he reached into a carved cubby in the ice wall and tossed a little box at her. She glanced at it and laughed. He'd given her a deck of cards.

"Is this your way of saying you'd like to play strip poker?"

His jaw dropped. A very square jaw, she should add, the man being all chiseled sharp edges, thick but not fat, and strong she'd guess, given what she'd seen of his body. Handsome. if you liked the rugged, grumpy type.

Her lips quirked. "Guess there's not much sport in strip poker at this point seeing as how you already saw me in my nude glory."

"I didn't gawk, if that's what you're insinuating," he muttered. "Who do you think covered you in a blanket?"

"Speaking of blanket, where should I sleep?" The little girls had a single bed in their room, which they shared. The living room had a large chair carved in stone as well as smaller ones.

He stared at her. "I don't have a guest room."

"Guess it will be a chilly night, then." She grimaced as she eyed the floor. Even with the wolf rug, it would be cold. She'd have to shift shapes, or she'd never sleep.

His head tilted back, and the mightiest sigh exited him as he muttered, "You can sleep with me."

"Why, Nookie, I thought you weren't interested," she teased.

"My bed is large enough we don't have to touch."

"What, no cuddling?" She couldn't help taunting

and couldn't have said why. Maybe because his cheeks turned a ruddy color? He might be a grouch, but he was still a man, and she a woman. A woman who'd not been with someone in a while.

"Don't make me change my mind," he warned.

"I'll be a good reindeer," she promised, crossing her fingers behind her back.

"Come on, then." He lumbered into the large bedroom and pulled back the thick fur-lined blanket. Another plush layer sat atop his rock-framed bed.

"You'll sleep on that side." He pointed to the left.

She clambered in, keeping on his oversized clothes even though she usually slept nude at home. Then again, in her cabin, she had a woodstove constantly emitting heat.

Despite the blankets, she shivered, the cold radiating through the bottom sheet. The bed didn't creak or move as Nanook joined her.

Being a man, he quickly fell asleep. Breathing evenly, not snoring as expected. He also emitted heat. She could feel it despite the foot of space between them. It drew her. She scooched closer, basking in the warmth, and fell asleep wondering what she'd do to help Santa and those being held hostage in the village.

Dancer woke in the morning, plastered across a bear.

A bear with a hard-on.

And what did she just have to say? "Is that a pogo stick in your pants, or are you happy to see me?"

4

With a shiver and a sigh, the naked lady woke,
But the true shock came when she spoke.
It's an emergency, a calamity, she told us right then,
Santa's been taken prisoner and Christmas is ruined.

The bear didn't care and wanted to toss her out,
But for once, he didn't loudly shout.
He did, however, say, don't you dare squeal,
Or I might decide you're tastier than a fat seal.

NANOOK WOKE from a strange dream where a reindeer showed up to his cave claiming Santa's Village had been invaded. Only it turned out to be real, seeing as how a woman lay splayed across him, sleeping.

It had been a while since he'd shared his bed, or cuddled, and to his surprise, he didn't hate it. On the contrary, rather than dump Dancer on her rump, he allowed himself to enjoy having someone touching him, a tad too much as it turned out because, when she woke, squirming atop him, his dick roused as well.

And she noticed.

At least she didn't ask if he had a pencil. A pogo stick was a respectable size. Still, the whole situation embarrassed, so he made it even worse.

"Move," he grumbled. "Gotta pee."

"Mmm, do you have to?" She burrowed against his chest. "You are deliciously cozy."

Tempting, but no. "Get off."

"If I must," uttered melodramatically as she slid to the side.

He exited the bed, and she immediately nestled in the warm spot he left behind. By the time he returned from doing his business, the twins were in bed with Dancer, and before he could stop them, Sesi asked, "Are you our new mommy?"

Dancer blinked. "Uh, no."

"But you're in Dada's bed," Siku pointed out.

"Auntie Kira and Uncle Arnie sleep in the same bed because they're a mommy and daddy." Sesi wasn't giving up.

"Sometimes grownups share to be kind. In this case, your Dada didn't want me to sleep on the floor," Dancer replied.

"You could have slept with us. I would have shared my pillow," Siku offered.

Dancer kindly turned down the offer. "How sweet of you. But your Dada had more room in his bed. I wouldn't want to squish you."

Siku whispered to her sister, "She's not a good bed sharer. I saw her on top of Dada, smushing him."

It led to Sesi pursing her little mouth. "Maybe it is better you sleep with Dada."

Nanook almost choked.

"I'm hungry. What about you?" Dancer asked, changing the subject.

"Yes! I like porridge for breakfast," Sesi declared.

"Blech. Pancakes are better." Siku made a face.

"Only when we have syrup."

"Jam is yummy on them too," Sesi insisted.

"I usually have granola and yoghurt," Dancer commented.

"What's that?"

"Granola is oats mixed with nuts and honey, sometimes a bit of coconut. Yoghurt is like a milk pudding. Peach-flavored is my favorite," Dancer explained to her avid audience.

"What's a peach?" Siku questioned. They didn't have access to much fruit. Mostly canned stuff, which he rarely bought. Polar bears were mostly meat eaters.

"Stop pestering our guest," he stated, finally interjecting.

"But, Dada, she's interesting," whined Sesi.

Indeed, she was, hence why she had to go. "Storm cleared up overnight."

Dancer arched a brow. "Is that a hint to get trotting?"

Before he could stop himself, he said, "I'll give you a ride. Girls, eat your breakfast and then get geared up while I prep the sled."

Dancer popped out of bed. "Really? You'll take me to FARTZ?"

He nodded. "I can trade for supplies as well as scout out where to build our new home when we move."

"Thank you!" To his shock, she flung her arms around his neck and hugged him tight.

His cock—which he'd just beaten to death in the lavatory—sprang back to life.

Luckily, she didn't stay plastered long enough to notice. "I'm going to have a little nibble with the girls. Then I'll give you a hand readying to go."

Before he could say *Don't need a hand*, she'd flounced off and he stood there wondering what possessed him.

Kindness?

Nah.

More like an urgent need to get the woman far away from him. She had him feeling things he'd rather not deal with. Attraction, amusement, intrigue. All emotions that led to him being burned the last time.

Best he rid himself of her, but even he wasn't so heartless as to send her out on her own on foot—or hoof. The northern part of Ellesmere Island could be treacherous to the unknowing.

When the time came to leave, he offered Dancer an old wolf fur cloak to wrap around her, as well as two more pairs of socks for her feet since he didn't have anything that would fit her slender arch. The pull-along had enough room for her to ride with the girls, but then he couldn't bring some of the whale and seal meat he'd been planning to use for trade.

A dilemma unless...

"You'll ride on the sled behind me," his gruff order.

"Okay." She didn't argue.

He loaded the trailer with bundles, and the girls tucked themselves in amongst them with their thick blanket. They'd have been warm enough as cubs, but every year, more and more humans chose to explore with their damnable cameras. The last one who'd seen him with a pair of polar cubs took issue and accused him of illegally trapping an endangered species. He couldn't exactly tell the guy they were his kids, so he'd fabricated a story about their polar bear mother dying and him fostering them until they got big enough to head out on their own.

When the guy kept harping, he suffered an unfortunate accident. Happened quite a bit to the tourists around here and yet they kept coming.

When the time came to leave, Dancer straddled the sliver of seat left at his back and wrapped herself around him, a reminder not to fart. He'd held one in that morning in bed as well. Maybe if he'd let it rip, she wouldn't have been so keen on cuddling.

They set off, moving fast, his snowmobile powerful enough to pull all their weight and still maintain a decent speed on the flat spots, of which there weren't many. He'd chosen to live in the mountainous area as opposed to the plains where the FARTZ encampment sprang up.

The chill wind had Dancer tucking her face into his back. A good idea since he didn't have a spare set of goggles for her.

The encampment was an hour away technically, but he only made it that fast when he had daylight. This time of year, in the pitch-black, he had to drive carefully, lest a new hazard catch him by surprise. Technically, Dancer could have trotted to FARTZ. After all, reindeer could run up to fifty miles per hour and handle the cold. However, navigating the ruts would have been challenging. She could have easily twisted or broken a leg. Not to mention, a reindeer alone might prove tempting for any roaming predators, hence the offer to escort her.

Look at him thinking of someone other than his girls for once. Was he softening in his old age? No, but he also wasn't a complete dick. While he hated Santa's Village, more specifically the elves, he felt somewhat chagrinned at the idea of kids having their Christmas ruined. He might not celebrate, but he still recalled that wide-eyed wonder of booking it downstairs to see what Santa placed under the tree.

Had it been wrong of him to deprive his girls of that pleasure? Then again, Santa, that sneaky bastard, had found ways to leave them stuff. Unwrapped boxes left outside his cave. The girls always assumed their father had gotten them a surprise. Never mind the fact the encampment didn't sell toys or the stuffies his girls adored. Santa made sure his good girls got rewarded, and this despite the fact he didn't get credit for it. Maybe he'd been too harsh banning the big man completely.

The ride from the mountain to the camp proved uneventful. Not a single living thing spotted, which was kind of odd. Probably still hunkering down from the storm.

Nanook parked his sled by a premade capsule house, the newest gimmick in building innovation. There were several in the camp now, practical designs that could be preassembled, transported, and dropped into place. At a cost, of course. His sister had told him the price, and he'd calculated how many whales he'd have to harvest to pay for it.

A lot.

Doable, but did he really need a fancy place with stone counters, hidden storage, heated floors, and a fake fireplace? His sister did, and had upgraded to add a second pod to expand her living space so each kid had their own room. Except when Nanook visited. Then Peter had to bunk with Roger, which led to some screaming matches and wrestling. His daughters liked to watch and mutter, "Boys." Sounded just like their Aunt Kira.

His nephews emerged from their home in a blur of excited voices and limbs. "Uncle Nook, Sesi, and Siku are here!" they yelled, converging on the girls. While a few years older, they'd taken on the role of older brothers—which meant they taught his daughters how to misbehave.

Kira, Nanook's older sister, emerged and waved. "I'm surprised to see you here before the New Year."

"I had an unexpected visitor who needed a ride to town." As he spoke, Dancer peeled herself from his back and peeked out of the fur to smile and wave. "Hi."

"Welcome." His sister smiled, and right away, Nanook knew she got the wrong idea. "Come in. Come in. The more, the merrier."

"Yeah, Merry Christmas," screamed the boys.

Which was when it hit Nanook. He usually didn't visit in December for a very good reason.

And that reason was plastered all over his sister's home when they walked in.

Tinsel. Fluff. A fake tree hung in garland, shiny, colorful balls, and lights. On a shelf, a figurine of a fat man in a red suit holding a large sack.

The girls' faces lit up. "What's this?" they exclaimed, taking in all the gaudy decorations.

To her credit, his sister tried to respect his wishes. "It's for Christmas, a holiday we celebrate."

At the curious glances from his daughters, which screamed *why don't we*, he shrugged. "Not everyone partakes."

But that wasn't enough for his girls, and as they pestered asking questions, which his nephews happily answered, he scowled, deeper and deeper until Dancer murmured, "You wouldn't have been able to hide Christmas forever. Once they started school, they would have found out."

Something he now realized. Guess it might be time

to give up his grudge on the holiday, but he still reserved the right to eat elves.

Kira wrangled the twins out of their outer clothes and gave them snacks before planting herself in front of Nanook and Dancer with a curious expression. "My brother forgot to introduce us. I'm Kira, and you are…"

"Dancer Lightfoot, of Santa's Village. Second lead for his team of reindeer."

"I'm surprised to see you here this close to the big day."

"I had no choice. There was an emergency. I need help," Dancer stated.

"How can we aid you?" Kira didn't hesitate.

The delicate reindeer glanced at the children admiring the tree and leaned close to Kira to whisper, "Santa and all his workers have been taken hostage. I need every volunteer we can muster to set them free and save Christmas."

5

Away from Santa's Village,
Without a single thread,
The brave reindeer Dancer,
Wanted to bang her sweet head...

The folks on the island
Made fun of her dread,
Yet, without their cooperation,
Santa could soon be dead.

DANCER DIDN'T EXPECT laughter when she announced the emergency in Santa's Village.

Kira couldn't stop chortling, and Dancer finally offered a stiff, "I'm not sure why it's so funny."

"Because Santa's Village is much too well defended to have been taken over by surprise. I mean the QUEEFS are pros at repelling attempts at penetration. Then you have the many elves who can be quite tricky to trap. Plus, there's the big man himself. He's killer with a sword."

"I don't know how, but Krampus somehow managed to overcome those defenses."

"Krampus?" Kira suddenly sobered. "He doesn't exist."

"Tell that to the person using that name. This Krampus got an army of wolverines and walrus to mount the coup." And who knew what else at their command.

"To do what?" Kira asked.

"Take over the village."

"Again, to do what?"

Dancer paused. "I don't know. I didn't stick around to ask."

"I mean, when you think about it, what could this Krampus possibly want with a remote village that makes toys?"

"Does the motivation really matter? We have to rescue them, or there won't be a Christmas."

"I'm not sure what we can do. We don't have any boats sturdy enough to handle the Arctic Sea this time of year," Kira murmured.

Transportation did pose an issue. "Honestly, we need an army, which is why my plan was to report what's happened to FUC HQ. They can dispatch whatever force is needed."

"We can try to call. However, the radios have been nothing but static the past few days. Arnie, my husband, says our dish isn't receiving or sending signals. Even the satellite phones aren't working."

Nanook rumbled. "What's causing the issue?"

"Geomagnetic storms. We've been clobbered by them recently. While inconvenient to our electronics, the resulting Aurora Borealis have been spectacular."

"This is bad," Dancer muttered. Her entire plan had hinged on contacting the proper authorities to handle the situation. Now she had nothing.

"Don't lose hope yet. There must be something we can do." Kira addressed her brother. "You're the ex-military guy. Any suggestions?"

"Military? I thought you were a FUC agent?" Dancer questioned.

"Technically both. I served in a Special Forces Polar Unit for a few years but retired when I met the twins' mother on a visit back home."

Kira's face darkened, and her lips pursed. "That two-timing wh—"

"She is the mother of the twins, so be careful what you say," he grunted, interrupting his sister.

Did Nanook still have feelings for her? Dancer had thought from what he'd explained earlier that he hated his ex, but now he defended her honor.

Kira sniffed. "I'm allowed to not like Anjij and what she did. Getting you to quit your career to work as a hunter for Santa's Village, only to decide that's not what she wanted, was selfish."

"I didn't mind settling down. I'm glad I did, or I would have missed out on the twins' milestones."

A man who put his children before his career. Nice. But even better, his past military experience might prove useful.

"Since you're the polar military expert, what do you suggest we do next?" Dancer asked.

"There is no we. I've done my part. Got you to FARTZ. Now the rest is up to you."

"But I don't know what to do," she huffed. "If I were in Greenland, I would have been able to dump this on the FUC garrison stationed there. They would have had the tools to launch a counterattack. Instead, I'm on Ellesmere Island, with no way of contacting anyone." Her lower lip jutted.

Nanook's mouth tightened. "A counterattack would get people needlessly killed."

"Then what? Just let Krampus keep the hostages, the village, and have Christmas ruined?" she huffed. "If I'd known no one would help, I would have stayed and seen if I could rescue them myself."

"You would have been captured," his blunt reply. "This is a job for professionals. A situation like this, what you want is a small task force that can go in and eliminate the main threat. Krampus' death would most likely throw the entire operation into chaos. Militant groups tend to disperse when they lose their leader."

He suggested the impossible. "Great idea, now I just need a team of assassins. Know where to find some?" her sarcastic rejoinder.

"I know of a sniper that might agree if you can get him sober for that long."

She perked up. "Really?"

Kira cleared her throat. "Actually, Benedict's been clean for more than three months now."

"Good for him," Nanook stated and glanced at

Dancer. "Before you ask, I'll take you to see him after I get the sled unloaded."

"I'll help."

"No, you won't. That's man's work," Nanook snapped as he headed outside.

Her brows raised. "Is he always that sexist?"

Kira grinned. "On some things, yes. It's kind of cute. When he's around, I never have to carry a thing. Wish Arnie were the same way. He's too progressive though. Says anything he can do, I can probably do better. I think that's just his way of avoiding taking out the trash."

"Is your husband as grumpy as your brother?"

"No, thank bearness. Nook didn't used to be so grouchy, but the breakup with the twins' mother really affected him."

"Yeah, we heard about it in the village. Rough thing to have happen."

"It's why he hates Christmas so much. Meanwhile, it's not the holiday that's to blame," Kira pointed out.

"At least his daughters adore him."

"Because he dotes on them. Not in a spoil-them-rotten kind of way but in how he listens to them, pays attention, spends time with them."

"He's a hunter, though. Doesn't that mean he leaves them alone quite often?"

Kira shook her head. "He never hunts far or long. He's quite efficient at it. When they were younger, he used to bring them with him and keep them tucked in the sled. But now they're of an age where they can spend a few hours entertaining themselves."

Unlike humans, shifters understood their young needed to learn independence at a tender age. In the wild, they never knew when a predator or threat might take them out, so it was important a young cub, pup, fawn etcetera knew how to cope.

"Who's this Benedict you were mentioning?"

"Old friend of Nanook's. They served together in the military. Nanook retired for his family, and a few years later, Benedict got a medical discharge. Injured wing meant he couldn't fly anymore. Hit him pretty hard. He'd spent the last two years constantly drunk, although I do have to commend him for brewing his own noxious alcohol to do so."

"And you think he can help?" A former alcoholic didn't seem like the best choice in such a dire situation.

"Benedict's a crack shot. His snow-owl roots mean he's got excellent eyesight. Add in natural skill, and he can shoot the whisker off a seal in motion."

Impressive if true. Could it be as simple as shooting this Krampus to free the village?

If there was anything left to free. The snowman screaming as he melted haunted her. How many had died in the invasion? Did Santa even still live, or had Krampus eliminated his greatest threat? And then there was the question of, even if this Benedict agreed, how would they get there? She could only hope Nanook had a solution for that. Even better, that he'd change his mind and would join them, too. A polar bear on their side would even the odds.

It didn't take Nanook long to unload the sled, his sister making a list of the package contents and then writing down what he wanted in exchange. A place like this didn't deal in currency but in trade, kind of like Santa's Village.

Nanook went to speak to his girls for a moment before turning to Dancer. "Ready to go meet Benedict?"

She nodded. Kira proved kind enough to outfit her in something other than socks, loaning her some boots that were slightly too large but warm. She kept the wolf fur cloak; however, she did swap his massive garments for something from Kira's closet. Still loose but at least she didn't have to roll the cuffs a half-dozen times.

They emerged from the pod into light, the encampment having installed sources of illumination. Mostly fluorescents bolted to the roofs of homes or rising from columns planted in the ground, but many folks also had twinkling Christmas lights, their bright colors pleasing to the eye. A certain grumpy someone didn't view them the same way.

"Waste of electricity," he grumbled.

"Where do they get their power from?" she asked, not hearing the loud roar of generators. Santa's Village used a compact nuclear reactor, built by the elves and buried under the ice.

"Water turbines. There's plenty of fjords around, so someone built a mini hydroelectric facility.

"That can't have been cheap," she observed.

"It wasn't. However, given the military outpost in Alert, they managed to get some of it funded by the government and the rest from FARTZ backers."

"What exactly is this place? Why would someone give them money?" she queried.

"FARTZ is a research camp. At least on paper. In truth, while they do have a few scientists who study the arctic and the life around it, its primary purpose is food supplier to shifters. The amount of meat consumed by our kind would appear suspicious if bought from regular sources. Not to mention, whale and seal meat is outlawed in some areas, which is difficult for those of us originally from the north, as it forms an important part of our diet."

"Everyone in the camp is shifter?"

"Mostly. A few inter-marriages mean we have a couple residents who are fully human but aware of our secret. It's a safe place," he added. "You won't have to hide your horns here."

"I never realized there was a shifter-friendly town so close by, which sounds terrible, I'm sure, since we drop presents off each year." While she currently wore a woolly hat that covered her head and the horny nubs, it intrigued to know there was a place other than Santa's Village that might be accepting of her difference.

"It being a shifter-safe zone is why the girls will be going to school here." He pointed as they passed a mobile trailer. "There's only about twenty kids and two teachers, but they're good ones. Or so Kira says. Those who want a diploma that's recognized by colleges and universities simply have to write an exam to showcase their knowledge."

"Did you grow up here?"

He shook his head. "Originally from Alaska but I was posted for a while in Alert while in the military."

"So how did you end up at Santa's Village?" She knew because of Kira but wanted to hear it from him.

He sighed. "Are you ever going to stop asking questions?"

"Probably not."

She thought he wouldn't reply, but after a pause, he rumbled, "I met my wife while serving in Alert. When they would have sent me overseas without her, I chose to resign my commission. My sergeant at the time, an arctic fox from the area, was the one to suggest Santa's Village. They needed someone to hunt for fresh meat. Given Anjij was pregnant, it seemed like a great place to raise our kids."

"But she wanted something more," she guessed.

"Yeah. Not that she ever told me. I never expected a polar bear, who thrives in snow and ice, to have such a deep hankering for the tropics."

"She could have travelled for a visit."

"That would have made the most sense, but instead, she decided me and the girls were holding her back from having her best life."

"If you ask me, she chose wrong. Those daughters of yours are an absolute delight."

He glanced at her with clear surprise. "You like kids?"

"You do remember where I work, right?" her dry reply.

"You pull a sleigh. Doesn't mean you like ankle-biters."

"I do, though. Hoping one day to have some of my own, but that would require meeting someone who isn't repulsed by my horns." Rejection hurt, especially for something she couldn't change.

"Why would they be repulsed?" He sounded genuinely surprised.

"I'm considered defective among the herd. No one wants to mate with someone who might give them less-than-perfect kids." Her lips turned down. "Only Santa saw past my appearance and gave me a job."

"You like it? The whole flying him around for Christmas?"

"The flying part yes, but the man is a task master. The training is quite rigorous."

"I don't know how you do it. Never did like heights," he admitted.

"And for me, I'm not big on swimming. Too many things that want to bite my legs." She shuddered. She'd had an uncle emerge three-legged from a polar dip.

"Ain't much trying to chew on me," he drawled.

She almost said something wildly inappropriate because he seemed very edible to her. "I don't imagine there are many things that would mess with an ice bear."

"Only the dumb ones. We're here," he suddenly stated, their stroll having brought them to a strange abode. Set upon concrete stilts perched a house. A ladder led up to it.

"This is where he lives?" she asked, craning to look upward.

"Yeah. He likes having a bird's-eye view." Nanook tilted his head and bellowed, "Benny. You up there?"

It took only a moment before a head popped out of a

hatch in the floor of the house. "Nanook? I'm surprised to see you here this close to Christmas."

"Extenuating circumstances," he groused. "Can we speak for a moment?"

The man's gaze strayed to Dancer, and his brows rose. "By all means. Come on up."

Nanook gestured at her to go first. She gripped the ladder and climbed, about twenty feet or so she figured. The hatch remained open, and she slipped into a cozy place. She looked around as Nanook clambered up next.

The place appeared made of some plastic-like substance, obviously insulating since the small stove managed to keep it warm. There wasn't much in the way of furnishing. A single bed tucked against a wall. Two chairs, a plain wooden one and a fabric-covered one. A table. A shelving unit holding books, as well as cans and boxes of food. A counter with a sink had dishes underneath. No bathroom. Must make for chilly bathing and other urgent business.

The man who owned the house appeared just as sparse. Lean compared to Nanook, his sandy-blond hair shaggy. His eyes hazel, leaning toward golden yellow. He wore a woollen knit sweater and jeans.

Nanook squeezed through the slim hatch, grumbling, "Damned thing keeps shrinking."

"Must be, because you certainly haven't put on any winter pounds," was Benedict's dry reply.

The comment earned him a glare then a smile, which transformed Nanook's face. "The hunting's been good thus far this season."

"It has been. That last batch of seal meat you brought was delicious. Have a seat," Benedict offered. "Can I get you something? Coffee? Tea?"

"Aren't you going to ask who the woman is?" Nanook countered.

"I figured you'd tell me when you were good and ready." Benedict filled a kettle and put it on his heating stove.

"Name's Dancer. She's from Santa's Village."

"Far from home," Benedict remarked, sitting himself in the worn recliner covered in a blanket.

"Not by choice," she mentioned. "The village was attacked. Santa and the elves captured."

Benedict's brows rose. "Attacked by who? Did the humans finally pierce the protective veil hiding it?"

No one knew how it worked exactly. Santa never revealed his secrets. However, one could only assume super advanced technology, given those flying overhead couldn't see it, satellites never spotted it, and regular folk never stumbled across the village.

"Not humans. Krampus and an army of walrus and wolverines."

Benedict stared at her. She had remained standing, and Nanook took the only other chair, making it groan ominously.

"Say that again?" Benedict finally said.

"Krampus took over Santa's Village and imprisoned everyone."

"Krampus isn't real."

She rolled her eyes. "So everyone keeps saying. And yet, someone using that name attacked."

"You saw this Krampus?"

"No, but I did spot the army as it swept through the village. They exploded the paint factory, did something to the candy one as well. Possibly more damage was done after my departure."

"How unfortunate for the kids," Benedict murmured.

"Exactly, which is why we're here. We need your help."

Once more he stared at her before saying slowly, "Help how?"

"By taking out the leader of the invasion," she stated.

"And you came to me for help?" Benedict sounded incredulous.

"Nanook says you're a sharpshooter."

"Was. I haven't fired a gun since I retired from the military."

"Oh." She bit her lower lip. "Isn't it like riding a bicycle?" A skill once learned never forgotten.

"I don't know."

"Will you help?" she asked.

"Is she serious?" Benedict addressed Nanook.

"Very."

Benedict frowned at the polar bear. "It was your idea to bring her here? You know I don't do those kinds of missions anymore since my accident."

"It's for a good cause," Nanook pointed out.

"So, you're going on this mission?"

Nanook didn't reply, and Benedict snorted. "Didn't think you were. So, who all is going?"

"Me," Dancer replied.

"And?"

"You?" She added a questioning note.

"Not likely. Sounds like a suicide mission."

Her stomach sank. "Something must be done."

"Agreed. But you need more than a has-been. You should be mustering some FUC agents at the very least or, if you could get in touch with the right people, a special strike force."

"I would love to do that," she exclaimed, flinging her hands. "But none of the gingersnapping phones are working."

"Yeah, the magnetic storms have been fierce this past week. They'll come back online eventually."

"By then it will be too late. Christmas will be over. Children will be disappointed. Santa and his elves could even be dead!"

She was on the verge of tears and uttered a squeak as Nanook yanked her hard enough she fell into his lap, and then he wrapped his arms around her.

"Hush now," he rumbled. "You're getting overwrought."

His words countered the pleasure she got from being cuddled. "I'm upset because my home has been taken over and no one seems to care."

"We care. We just aren't the right people to fix it."

"But you're all I have," she whispered.

"Even if I wanted to help," Benedict stated, "I have no way of getting there. I can't fly anymore." He pointed to his bum arm.

Her lips turned down. "Neither can I. I ran out of Santa's dust."

"Meaning you'd need a boat or a plane to cross the sea. Both things we don't currently have. Although, Alert might have something."

"I see. Sorry to have disturbed you." She shoved out of Nanook's warm lap and headed for the ladder.

"Where are you going?" he asked.

"To find some people who aren't so caught up in their own self-misery that they can't see or act past it," she snapped, finally losing her peppermint-loving temper.

The men glared at her.

She didn't care.

"Enjoy marinating in your pity," she huffed.

With that, she left. And by left, she meant she hit the ground and started walking. Walked away from the FARTZ that left her with a sour taste. Away from the bear who hated Christmas. Into the cold unknown, in the direction of the next outpost.

If no one would help her save Santa's Village, then she'd just have to do it herself.

6

Joy to his world, the reindeer's gone,
Now Nanook can enjoy his peace.
Let his life go back to normal,
Meaning ice and snow will sing.
And again, ice and snow will sing—off-key
Oh, yes, ice and snow will drive him to drink.

"DANCER IS cute when she's pissed," Benedict observed.

Yeah, she was. "Hadn't noticed."

"Liar."

"I'm not looking to date," Nanook muttered.

"Maybe you should. Although you might need to apologize first. She's peeved." Benedict pointed out the obvious.

"Just a little."

"She can't have seriously expected us to go on a

mission to save Santa. I mean you hate Christmas, and I'm a broken drunk."

"I hear you've been sober for the past few months," Nanook remarked.

"I have, but I still get the cravings to get shit-faced. Which is why I can't do this. She deserves someone less messed up."

"There is no one else," Nanook replied. "At least not anyone close enough to make a difference."

"Guess Christmas is screwed this year. Once FUC finds out, I'm sure they'll give a hand."

"Will they?" Nanook queried. "Santa isn't a shifter. He simply employs some of our kind."

"FUC will want to save them."

"You know as well as me it will depend on the cost." And he didn't mean the monetary kind. Lose a few reindeer or lose some trained agents. Someone would have to make a hard choice.

"I'm sure they'll have a solution that's better than a crippled has-been."

Hearing Benedict disparage himself had Nanook growling. "You're not a has-been. Even if you can't fly, you could have helped."

"Said by the guy who also bailed and has been hiding in his cave these past few years."

"My situation is different."

"Yeah, it is, and you're being an even bigger whiner than me. You're not the first guy whose wife stepped out on him. But rather than deal with it, you've been sulking and pretending to hate everyone."

"Not pretending," Nanook interjected.

"You used to tolerate folks just fine before. I mean don't get me wrong. You were never super outgoing, but you used to be the kind of guy you could call at the last minute and ask for a ride home or to move some furniture. Used to be somewhat social but now you're the worst kind of recluse."

"Not for long. I'm moving back to town in the spring."

"Only because of the girls. I've seen you scouting the outskirts for a spot to set up. Looking to keep yourself apart."

Nanook sighed because his old friend wasn't wrong. "Guess we've both got our issues."

"We do," Benedict agreed.

And for some reason, he heard his sister's voice in that moment. Kira yelling at him when the girls started crying because they were leaving the camp to go back to their home, where they had no one but each other to play with. Kira had said, *"How long are you going to punish them because of something their mother did?"*

"I'm not punishing them," he'd retorted.

"You're also not doing them any favors. They need people, Noonoo." Her pet name for him. *"Need to socialize and make friends. Not to mention, you deserve, make that need, to move on and find a way to be happy."*

"Who says I'm not?"

"Can you honestly say you enjoy life?"

He couldn't, so rather than lie, he did what he'd been doing since Anjij left. He ran away.

Dancer was right. He was a coward, a harsh realization that stung more than a jellyfish touching his ball sac.

"Sorry I bothered you." Nanook rose to leave.

"It's not too late to make nice with your girlfriend."

"She's not my girlfriend," Nanook muttered as he glanced out the window and saw her striding quickly up the snow-packed street between habitats.

"In that case, maybe I should reconsider her demand," Benedict mused aloud. "Ain't many options for dating around here, and if I did manage to help, she'd probably look upon me favorably."

"What happened to you don't shoot people anymore for a living?"

Benedict shrugged. "Only because there's been no one that needed it."

"You're going to volunteer just to get her to like you?" For some reason, this bothered Nanook.

"Beats sitting in my tower moping. And I feel bad we both turned her down."

"You know how I feel about Christmas."

"Christmas, Santa, and even the other elves aren't to blame for what happened," Benedict pointed out. A fact Nanook understood. He just didn't like it because it was easier to fault a holiday than to recognize the problems in his relationship.

If he were truthful with himself, he'd seen it coming. Anjij had shown signs of discontent not long after the birth. Unlike some females, she'd lacked a maternal instinct. She'd often lamented how having the twins had ruined her chance to do something with her life.

Whereas Nanook became a father and immediately his whole world revolved around the mini versions of him.

"I think I liked you better drunk," he growled.

"Ah yes, because slipping in my pile of puke the last time was so much fun."

"Fine. I'm proud you're sober. But I could do without the guilt-tripping and lectures."

"You only hate it because it's making you reflect. Being sober means I've had time to do that as well. I'm still struggling with the fact I'll never fly again. Never feel the wind under my wings. But also starting to realize that I need to get past that and find other things that bring me joy."

"And have you found anything?" Nanook asked.

"Not yet, but I've only just begun coming out of my misery." Benedict paused. "You know what? Maybe this mission would be a good way of getting me back out there."

"Now you change your mind? You couldn't do it while Dancer was here?"

"She took me by surprise, and old habits die hard. But now that it's messing around in my head, I'm thinking this might be just the thing I need to remind myself I'm still useful."

"All righty then, I'll let her know."

"Good. Guess I'd better clean my gun." Benedict grinned, shedding years of misery. "I wonder how many chicks will throw themselves at me if I save Christmas."

Benedict could have all of them... except for Dancer.

For some reason, the idea of them together made Nanook want to roar.

He left Benedict's, crunching the icy path back to his sister's. He entered to find his girls watching cartoons with the boys, a treat since his cave didn't have power.

"Hey, Kira. Where's Dancer?"

His sister turned from the stove with a frown. "I thought she was with you."

"I kind of made her mad, and she left Benedict's. She didn't come here?"

Kira shook her head. Arnie walked in at that moment, carrying an armful of clothes, which included the wolf cloak he'd given Dancer.

"Look what I found on my way home. Aren't these your old boots?" Arnie asked, holding them up.

"Bloody narwhal. She took off," Nanook grumbled. Not completely unexpected. After the rejection, she must have decided she wasted her time with FARTZ. But she couldn't seriously be thinking of trotting all the way to Alert. It would take her a day at the very least, even if she could keep a steady gait all the way, which she couldn't, not with the obstacles and perils on the way.

"She went alone?" Kira held her wooden spoon tight. "Oh dear."

She eyed Nanook, and he knew what she wanted him to say. Knew he'd volunteer because he, too, couldn't stand the thought of her alone in the cold.

"I'll need a harness pack for some stuff and don't hold dinner," he stated.

"She can't be that far. Or is this your way of saying you can't run that fat ass as fast as you used to?"

"I run plenty fast," he grumbled. Just not quite as quick as a peeved reindeer.

In short order, his sister had some survival gear, which included clothes, packed in the bag with the special straps that could be worn while in his bear shape. He didn't take the sled because the noise, not to mention the fumes, would mask Dancer's trail. He'd have to do this old school, using his nose and other polar senses that usually came in handy on a hunt.

His girls didn't seem bothered one bit their Dada was leaving. They barely turned their faces from the screen to give him a kiss.

Soon he was on his way, heading first to the spot where Arnie claimed to have found the clothes and picking up Dancer's tracks from there. He moved quickly, had to, because he could see she'd been using long strides to get away from FARTZ.

It took him over an hour to catch up to her and only because she'd paused to glance at the sky, which put on quite the glowing display of green lights. Always pretty, and it never got old.

Nanook chuffed as he neared, and she didn't turn her head. What if he'd been a real polar bear? She'd have been eaten.

She kept ignoring him as she stared at the sky.

It bothered, so he shifted, uncaring of the cold, and he bellowed, "What are you thinking going off by yourself?"

No reply because she didn't shift, and he had to wonder if she worried about frostbite. "I brought some clothes." He opened the pack and pulled out the heavy fur cloak, draping it over her before throwing on his insulated socks and his jacket, which came down mid-thigh. It cut some of the cold, but he wouldn't be able to stay in this shape for long without adding more layers.

Dancer shifted and hugged the cloak around her, its length enough she could stand on its hem to keep her feet from sticking to the ice.

"Now, care to explain yourself?" he huffed.

"Explain what? You made it pretty clear you wanted to be rid of me. I thought you'd be happy."

"Well, I'm not," he complained. "You can't go trotting into the wild because you're pissed."

"You're right. I should have found myself a nice cave to sulk in."

Ouch. Deserved. But still ouch. "I'm not in my cave now."

"Why are you here?"

"Because maybe, just maybe, I was hasty in refusing to help."

"Help how? You said it yourself. There's no boat or plane. No way to get back to the North Pole."

"Not entirely true," he muttered.

"Meaning what?"

"You seem to have forgotten I know where to find a helicopter."

"I thought you said this Charlie fellow who owns it was expensive."

"He is. But he's also former search and rescue. Retired a few years back and bought the decommissioned chopper he used to pilot to ferry around tourists."

"Aren't those the big ones meant to withstand all kinds of weather?"

He nodded.

"Meaning I should have skipped the FARTZ and gone straight to him." She glared at Nanook.

It might have been more effective if she weren't so blubbering cute.

"He might not have answered. Charlie ain't exactly the social type."

"He must be related to you then."

"Ha. Ha."

"Where is this Charlie and his helicopter?"

"About halfway between FARTZ and Alert. He lives in an abandoned hunt camp close to the shoreline."

"How do I get there?"

"By coming back with me to FARTZ so we can properly outfit ourselves and grab Benedict."

"Benedict made it clear he wasn't going to help."

"He changed his mind after you left."

She sighed. "Men."

"Yeah, yeah, we're rabbit turds. So, what do you say, Dani? Do you still want our help?"

"Dani?"

"Dancer makes me think of a ballerina. Never liked that prancing-around-in-tights stuff."

Her lips twitched. "Very well. I accept your offer, Nookie."

His turn to stare. "Uh, no."

"What's wrong? I thought we'd reached the point where we were giving each other nicknames."

"I want a better one. Like Ferocious. Or Icey."

"It's either Nookie or Wookie."

"Do I look like a giant walking carpet?" he complained, knowing she'd just compared him to Chewbacca.

"Well, you do sound like him. All hooting and honking. And you're pretty hairy."

"Normal hairy," he retorted.

"Says you."

His lips pinched. "Why must you vex me?"

"Because it's helping me deal with my stress."

"Oh." Still… "Can't you find another method? I'm trying to be nice."

"I think your idea of nice needs work."

He snorted. "Only if I planned to keep using it once you were gone."

"So, this is a special nice just for me?"

"Yes, so don't go telling anyone how kind I am. I'd hate to disappoint them with my fists and insults."

For some reason, her lips curved in amusement. "Your secret is safe with me, Nookie."

"Should we head back? Kira's got some stew on the stove."

"Mmm. I am hungry. I kind of left with no supplies."

"Let's get this stuff back in the knapsack and head back."

"How will you get it on if we're shifted?" she asked.

"I put it on beforehand and pray it's sitting right so it doesn't bust when I polar out."

"Or I could strap it on you before I shift."

"I don't want you freezing your delicate bits."

She snorted. "I'm not as fragile as you think. I live in the North Pole."

"And? You're just a tiny little thing."

She arched a brow. "Only you would think that. I am five foot ten, two hundred and ten pounds."

"Like I said, tiny."

"Spoken by the giant," she muttered. "What are you, six foot six?"

"Six foot eight, actually, and a solid three fifty." And fit, despite what his sister said about his ass.

"Okay, let's get this done. I'm eager to try that stew." As he stripped and stuffed his items in the pack, she cocked her head and glanced to the sky. "Do you hear that?"

"Hear what…" He paused in his packing and listened. It took a moment for his brain to register the oddity and mutter, "Is that bells?"

"Reminds me of Santa's sleigh," she murmured, gaze trained overhead. "But Christmas isn't for a few more days."

An ominous feeling hit. "We need to get back, now." He snagged her cloak and stuffed it in the pack, feeling a need to rush, even as he knew they were at least an hour away from the camp. But out here, no one abandoned useful things, especially not winter gear.

He shrugged on the pack, his body tightening in the

cold. Dani hadn't yet shifted. She stared at the sky and whispered, "Do you see what I see?"

A lift of his gaze to the sky had him blinking, but the image didn't change. A sled coursed across the sky, illuminated by the Aurora Borealis lights. A massive sleigh like Santa used, only it wasn't drawn by flying reindeer.

"Are those wolverines?" he asked with a tone of incredulity.

"Yes, and judging by their flight path, they're heading for FARTZ."

His eyes widened. "My girls." His family. He didn't say another word but shifted, his pack managing to stay on during the transition. He began running back to the camp, outpaced by the reindeer that bolted past him. What took an hour was shortened to forty-five minutes, but it was still too long.

By the time they arrived, the camp was quiet, too quiet. Probably because everyone was asleep.

Franko lay on the ground snoring, still clutching the fish he'd been bringing home.

Mrs. Tiddles sat slumped in her doorway, letting the cold air inside her pod.

He raced to his sister's place and arrived after Dancer, who'd gone inside. As he entered, he found her looking pale and shaken.

A quick glance showed his sister and Arnie at the kitchen table, slumped over, sleeping. Of the girls or his nephews, he saw no sign.

He still called for them. "Sesi, Siku!"

"They're gone," Dani murmured.

"They can't be gone." He refused to entertain the

thought. His precious babies probably visited someone or—

She held up a single strand of hair. Wolverine fur to be exact.

And he didn't need her saying, "Krampus took them," to know his daughters were in trouble.

7

> Oh, come all ye faithful, bring your guns
>   and ammo.
> Oh, come ye, oh come ye to rescue some
>   kids.

"THIS IS YOUR FAULT! I should have been here protecting my cubs, not chasing after you," Nanook roared, which didn't have the effect he wanted seeing as how he was standing, naked, gloriously so, his rage making his balls jingle and his cock jangle.

She kept her gaze on his face. "Do you think it would have mattered? Or did you not notice everyone is asleep?" She swung her hand to indicate his sister and her husband, lying face first in their dinner. "They gassed the whole town, most likely with the same stuff Santa uses to blanket cities and towns so no one spots him on his run."

"I would have fought it off!" he declared.

"No one can unless you've been given the antidote."

Which wore off after a few days. All the reindeer took a dose before their Christmas ride.

"This can't be happening. This is my fault. I should have never left the cave."

"So, your girls would have been perhaps spared but not everyone else's kids. Your nephews are missing too."

He glared at her. "I'm aware. Your point?"

"The point is now we have to act. Even if your girls hadn't been taken, can you really say you wouldn't have helped your sister get her boys back?"

"Of course I would have. I might not be a social bear, but I'm not a goat's butthole."

"We need to move fast, especially since we don't know why Krampus took the children."

"What if it plans to eat them?" Nanook suddenly shrank in on himself.

"Don't think like that." She reached out and put a hand on his arm.

"Why else would that *thing* take them?"

"We don't know, and freaking yourself out won't help."

He paced, bouncing his dick with his angry stride. She averted her gaze.

"I need to get to Charlie. He'll fly us over, and I will tear Krampus to pieces," Nanook declared, slamming a fist into his palm.

"Excellent plan, but maybe we should bring more than just an angry ice bear."

"I'm worth ten foes," he growled. "Twenty when I'm pissed."

"And Krampus has more than that in that army I told you about. You said Benedict changed his mind? We should bring him along. Anyone else good with a gun?"

"I know a few. But they're all asleep." He waved his hand. "How long until they wake up?"

"Not long. An hour at most and given we spent part of that traveling, they should be waking up shortly. While we wait, let's get packing for the trip."

Before they could start, Kira began to rouse, lifting her face from her bowl of stew, licking her lips before opening her eyes and mumbling, "I must have been more tired than I thought."

"You were drugged so Krampus could take the kids!" Nanook announced without preamble.

The claim fully woke Kira, who sprang to her feet and roared, "My babies!"

It led to Arnie stirring next. "What's wrong, my chonky wife?"

"Someone took the boys."

"And my girls," Nanook added.

"What?" Arnie popped up from the table and began to bulge, his polar side reacting to the news.

"Hold on." Dancer waved her hands. "Before you go charging outside, they're not here."

"They can't have gone far," Arnie growled.

"Actually, they can since their abductors came by air."

"Air? The kidnappers flew?" Kira asked with a creased brow.

"Kind of. Krampus used Santa's sled pulled by some flying wolverines."

The claim stunned Kira and Arnie into silence.

Nanook's face turned icy and hard. "So, here's what we're going to do. Kira, I need you to find Rook and Weaver. Tell them to bring all their guns. Arnie, you're fetching Benedict. Make sure he's got his tripod and scope. Also, we'll need sleds to transport everyone."

"How will a sled catch them if they've been taken to the North Pole?" Kira cried, clasping her hands.

"They won't, but they'll get us to Charlie."

Their faces went from confused to understanding and determined. "Who else should I grab?" Arnie asked.

"Charlie's chopper can hold up to fourteen people, including the pilot. Although, given the size of some of us, a safer number of passengers might be ten," commented Nanook.

"So, Rook, Weaver, me, you, Charlie, Benedict, that's five. Four polar bears, a caribou, and a flightless owl. Who else?"

"Me," Dancer announced. "I might not be able to shoot, but I know the village."

"I'm going as well," Kira declared. "And don't you dare say no to me. They have my boys. Those wolverines are going to make great carpets by the time I'm done with them."

"So that puts us at seven. Who else?" Nanook asked.

The other three selected were Gertie, who could pick locks. Leroy, who was a snow goose and could provide

DANCER AND THE ICE BEAR

aerial reconnaissance. And to round it off, Felicia, an arctic fox who could get into tight spaces.

Within the hour, they were loaded and ready to go. Dancer rode behind Nanook, arms wrapped around his solid frame. The sledge they pulled was loaded with supplies.

Benedict doubled behind Gertie but only after complaining, "Riding bitch! How emasculating." Arnie and Kira each had their own ride. Leroy shared with Felicia, and Rook took Weaver on his snowmobile. Their large party took off, watched in silence by those who'd lost children but wouldn't be coming on the rescue mission.

How horrible for them to wake to their progeny gone, but she noticed how many of them stiffened their upper lips—and showed teeth—when Nanook gave a short speech.

"I'll get the kids back and will eat the heart of the bastard who took them!"

Violent, to the point, and kind of inspiring.

Despite her initial impression of the man, she'd come to see there was a depth to Nanook. A father who would do anything for his kids. A loner who retained strong family ties. A sense of honor, coming after her because he feared she'd get into trouble A reluctant hero... Oh and a stud.

In the past, Dancer had only really dated other reindeer. She didn't have many choices in Santa's Village. The elves were too fragile for a woman her size and strength. Whereas the visitors and other folks who'd passed through seemed to gravitate to the more delicately sized females.

But Nanook saw her as a woman. Had been visibly aroused by her presence. What a pity his ex-wife had ruined him for relationships, not that he'd be even contemplating one with his twins in danger. Currently, he focussed on rescue, and that meant she had to get her antlers straight. Once they reached the North Pole, they'd need a plan of action. Krampus would most likely have sentries watching. They had no idea what kind of numbers to expect. Not to mention, they'd have to be cautious lest the innocents get caught in the crossfire, which led to her wondering why Krampus had taken the children in the first place—and if they were still alive.

As they travelled, the sky remained a glowing green, the lights swirling and shifting, illuminating the snow while, at the same time, messing with visibility. Arnie's sled hit a rut and snapped a ski, forcing him to double up on his wife's sled, but that was their only hiccup.

They pulled up outside Charlie's place, a large hangar with no windows and a single person-sized door, if one ignored the massive bay door blocked by a snow drift.

Nanook rapped and waited.

No reply.

He pounded harder, and a faint grumbling was heard from within. "Calm your fucking teats. I'm coming."

The door opened to reveal a grizzled man, his white hair standing on end, his beard and mustache just as messy. He squinted at Nanook. "I know you. Weren't you stationed at Alert?"

"Yup. Been a while."

"No shit. Your hair's kind of long for the military, or have their standards changed?"

"I retired. Just a civilian now."

"Says the guy who arrived at my door loaded with guns."

How could he tell? They were still packed on the sled.

"We need your help," Nanook stated.

"For what?" a suspicious Charlie asked. He'd yet to invite them inside.

"We need transport to the North Pole. Preferably within a mile of Santa's Village."

Charlie snorted. "No can do."

"Is the chopper broken?"

"Nope. It's in fine condition. Thing is, Santa and I have an understanding. I don't take lookie-loos near his territory, and in return, I get a case of Jack every year at Christmas."

"This is an emergency," Nanook exclaimed. "Our children have been taken, and we must secure passage to the North Pole to get them back."

"I'm sure if Santa took the kids, he had his reasons." Charlie went to close the door, but Dancer inserted herself.

"Excuse me, sir, but you said you have a deal with Santa."

"Yup. Going on twenty years now."

"A long time," she commented. "And such a shame it has to end."

"What are you talking about, girly?" Charlie's lips pursed.

"Santa's been taken prisoner. The village is under Krampus' control—"

"Krampus don't exist," Charlie interrupted.

"Someone using that name has invaded Santa's Village," she stated. "Given Santa's no longer in charge, that means no whiskey for you."

Charlie stared at her then glanced at Nanook. "She telling the truth?"

"Yeah."

"Well, then, that changes things. Guess my deal with the big guy is off. So, what were you saying about wanting to hire me for transport?"

"Hire?" Nanook blurted out.

"I don't work for free."

"But the children—"

"Aren't mine. And gas don't come cheap."

"We didn't bring money," Nanook admitted.

"What else you got?"

"Guns," Arnie stated, holding up a rifle.

"I got plenty of those," Charlie scoffed.

"I could bring you home-cooked meals once a week for the next year," Kira offered next.

"Don't need a chef. I got enough cans of beans to last me the next twenty years." Which explained the farty smell that wafted from the open door.

Those gathered eyed each other and shrugged. They'd not brought anything else.

DANCER AND THE ICE BEAR

Except for Benedict. "Don't worry. I came prepared." He sauntered over, a knapsack in his hand. He reached in and pulled out a cloudy bottle. "What about some moonshine?"

It led to Kira hissing, "I thought you'd gone sober."

Benedict glanced at her. "I am. Doesn't mean I dumped out my stash. I kept it for trading and just in case reality sucked."

"Moonshine, eh. I'd need more than a bottle," Charlie stated.

"I've got another half-dozen you can have if you give us a ride." Benedict tilted the bottle, making the liquid slosh.

Charlie licked his lips. "Is it potent?"

"Potent enough you'll freeze your dick off banging a snowwoman."

"Sold!" Charlie crowed.

Benedict handed over the bottle, but when Charlie would have guzzled some, Nanook growled. "You ain't flying us drunk. You drink after the drop-off."

"Spoilsport," grumbled the man. "And it ain't like we're leaving tonight."

"Why not?" Kira exclaimed. "My babies need their mama!"

"Because my equipment don't like those lights. So, unless you want to go for a swim, we wait until morning when they're gone."

Nanook didn't like the delay, no one did, but they wouldn't be much good if they crashed into the sea.

Despite the setback, they loaded the chopper with their gear to not waste time in the morning. Then they found spots in the cluttered hangar to curl up for some rest. Since they'd not brought sleeping gear—aka blankets—most chose to shift, their animal shape less prone to the cold and discomfort of a hard floor.

Dancer debated sleeping outside, as the snow might have been more comfortable. She kept tucking her spindly legs, squirming, twisting, but her discomfort kept her awake. Her agitation led to Nanook, in his bear shape. to grumble and reach out with a big paw.

He tugged her until she nestled against him then lay his leg over her, cocooning her, sharing the warmth of his body.

She finally fell asleep and woke, in her naked woman shape, splayed across his furry frame.

8

Two days before Christmas, a reindeer
   gave to me...
A massive boner that wasn't an urge
   to pee.

NANOOK DIDN'T MOVE, despite being awake. Dani slept, cuddled against his chest, completely nude. She'd shifted during the night and gone from tucked against his body to him wearing her like a blanket.

He wasn't sure how he felt about her doing that.

Horny, yes. He was a guy.

Comfortable, too. After all, she weighed nothing to him.

Confused, though, because he rather enjoyed her snuggling.

Then annoyed because someone farted loud enough she woke and stinky enough they all began to gag.

Charlie chuckled. "Maybe I should have accepted the offer of food other than beans."

Dani lifted her head, her eyes still sleepy and murmured, "I want to barf."

Not exactly a sexy good morning, not that he needed or expected one.

He chuffed and wiggled.

"Yes, I know, you need to pee," she stated, stretching and yawning. She sat up on his belly and reached for her clothes, shivering and complaining as she tugged on the cold garments, hiding her chilly skin. A pity because her naked body did make his morning brighter.

"I miss my stove. I keep my gear on a rack by it," she commented.

Nanook shifted, keeping his arm in his lap, lest his semi erection be noticed. "The girls like to sleep with their stuff under the covers."

"Because they're smart cookies." Dancer moved away to join Kira, who divvied out some rations. Even Charlie lined up for some of her homemade nut cake.

Nanook dressed and mentally prepared himself for the day ahead. Basically, he cleared his mind of the reindeer who kept trying to consume it.

There was nervous laughter and joking as they readied to leave. No one knew what to expect once they reached the North Pole. If they made it.

The chopper didn't appear to be in great shape. Duct tape on the body. Some bulky welded patches. A few knicks in the rotor blades.

Charlie saw him looking and sauntered close, hitching his pants. "She might not look pretty, but she's dependable."

"If you say so." Hard to take the man seriously, given his home appeared just as derelict.

"How do we get it outside?" he asked, eyeing the rusty hangar door that appeared sealed by ice to the floor.

"By going up." Charlie pointed overhead. Craning to follow the direction of the finger, Nanook could see the ceiling had a dual hatch, the sections mounted on hinges that would swing down when opened.

"You fly it out of your home?" Well, that certainly explained the mess.

"Can't exactly leave it outside," Charlie retorted. He turned a crank, and as the panels opened, snow drifted in. "Everyone aboard."

Everyone clambered into the chopper, which had been stripped on the inside, meaning no harnesses to hold them. A good thing the door on it closed. People chose a spot on the floor and sat. Nanook had his back against the rear wall and, without even thinking, tugged Dani to sit in his lap with his arms around her.

She peeked over her shoulder at him. "You trying to make sure I don't fall out?"

"Yup." Her excuse worked better than his, which was, *Don't know why I did it.*

The motor whined as Charlie flicked switches and got the blades turning. Weaver sat in only other seat beside their pilot, watching intently. He'd served in a different unit than Nanook and Benedict. Never told anyone why he asked to be discharged, but it must have been bad, as he often wore a haunted expression.

"Everyone ready?" Charlie shouted over the noise.

"Let's go save Christmas!" shouted Rook.

The chopper lifted, wobbling slightly, the whipping blades creating a tornado of wind inside the hangar, which made the messy space worse, if even possible.

They exited into the sky, still dark this time of year despite the morning hour. The chopper angled and headed for the edge of a cliff past which the dark and cold sea awaited.

Dani trembled slightly in his lap. Understandable, if this rickety hunk of metal went down, she'd drown, that was if she didn't die of hypothermia first. The polar bears in the group might survive. After all, swimming in cold water came second nature to them. However, even they would struggle if they crashed too far from shore.

Given the distance, depending on the speed, which appeared faster than expected, it would take them three to four hours to reach the North Pole. They spent that time discussing what they'd do once they arrived.

Kira was ready to march in and get her boys. "I will make soup out of any walrus that gets in my way," she promised.

Whereas Arnie, the calmer of the pair, stated, "Perhaps a frontal assault should be a last resort. The core mission is saving the kids, not packing our storage room with meat."

It was Nanook who reminded, "Taking out Krampus should be our primary objective. If we remove the fucker in charge, then there's a distinct chance the army will disperse without us having to fight."

"Where's the fun in that?" grumbled his sister, who was out for blood.

"Where do you think Krampus is holing up?" Benedict asked Dancer.

She shrugged. "There are a few places he might have chosen. Top pick would be Santa's house. It's the biggest home in the village and the most luxurious; however, it lacks defense. Which leads me to option two. Gingerbread Hall. The building was created to withstand catastrophe, whether it be a blizzard of the century or rampaging Yeti."

"Does that happen often?" Rook interjected.

"Not in my lifetime, but I've heard stories from some of the older elves. They call 1871 the Abominable Winter. Something like a dozen Yeti decided to raid the village. Stomped a good number of elves. Wrecked numerous structures and almost ruined Christmas."

Rook snorted. "Damn. That's wild. What happened to the Yeti?"

"Santa took them out with the help of some elves. After that incident, he created the QUEEFS," Dancer explained.

Kira snicked. "I can't believe no one saw a problem shortening their name."

"What's so funny about it?" Leroy asked.

Everyone ogled him, and Weaver said, "You don't know what a queef is?"

When Leroy shook his head, Weaver leaned over and murmured. Poor Leroy's eyes went wide and his cheeks red.

"Speaking of Santa's fighting force, do you think we can expect the elves to help?" Rook questioned.

"I don't see why they wouldn't," Nanook replied. "The question is, where are they being held and can they get their hands on weapons?"

"Assuming they're alive," Weaver's ominous addition.

Dancer murmured. "I didn't stick around long so can't really say for sure, but those wolverines that chased me definitely weren't playing nice. At the same time, the quick glimpse I got while flying away showed the walrus funneling the elves into Gingerbread Hall."

"If they're keeping them prisoner in the hall, expect it to be heavily guarded," Nanook rumbled.

"All of this chatter isn't really helping." Leroy joined the conversation. "Quite honestly, we can't make any kind of plans until we know the actual situation. Once we reach the North Pole, I'll fly over the village and do some reconnaissance. Once we know where Krampus is placed, along with troops and hostages, we'll be able to properly plot."

The snow goose had a point. Anything they decided now could change once they got paws on the ground.

Thump.

A minor impact had Kira shouting to Charlie, "What was that?"

"Bird. Flew right into me," their pilot yelled back.

Surprising, since it had to fight the wind from the rotors. Nanook thought little of it until the second and third impact. He slid Dancer to the side and plodded carefully to the cockpit. "What's happening?"

Charlie concentrated on flying but muttered, "More birds. Starting to think we're in the way of a migratory flock."

Unlikely, seeing as how they were close to the North Pole and seasonal birds would have long migrated.

"Any way you can see what's happening outside?" Nanook asked. The sky remained pitch-black, and Charlie had to guide using his navigational instruments.

"Rook, throw on the flood light."

Rook leaned forward and toggled a switch. A bright beam of light shot from the nose of the chopper, illuminating the space in front of them.

A space filled with birds.

Dozens, hundreds. Hard to count given the number of bodies being flung about, their wings caught in the draft caused by the chopper. The only clear thing?

"They're aiming for us," Nanook stated.

"Aye, they are," Charlie grunted. "Everyone, hold on tight. I'm gonna try and get us out of their path."

Nanook braced his legs and held the back of the pilot seats as Charlie tilted the whirly bird to the left and dropped them below the flock.

"That ought to do it," Charlie announced just as bird guts hit the windshield. More chunks coated the glass as the flock followed, suicide diving at the chopper from above.

"What in the cold Arctic Sea are they doing?" Charlie huffed. "They ain't acting normal."

Indeed, they weren't. The humming blades began to

whine as more and more birds threw themselves at the chopper. making it wobble.

"How far still? Nanook asked. They'd been flying for some time now.

"Not far," Charlie grunted. "Shore's still a few hundred yards."

Close, but not close enough.

Charlie fought to keep the chopper steady, but they wobbled. The birds kept bombing, some of them smashing into the windshield, hard enough it began to crack.

"Hold on, baby," Charlie pleaded. "You got this. Just a little farther."

A prayer dashed to pieces as the birds managed to jam the blades. The motor whined, but the rotor stopped turning. Without the spinning blades to keep them aloft, there was only one possible outcome.

They plummeted, and Nanook yelled, "Shift!" Because their human shapes would never withstand the impact and cold.

A tight space got even worse as the bears burst out of their clothes. Weaver chose to be smart. He slid open the door, letting in cold air before he leaped, changing into his bear midair.

A chonky polar-ized Kira jumped next, Arnie right behind her. They were close enough to the water the jump wouldn't hurt, and they could swim. Leroy turned into his snow goose and flapped away, the rest remained in the chopper when it hit the water, including a doe-eyed Dani.

Nanook shifted as the icy cold sea surged into the chopper, and he looked for his reindeer.

She'd made it out of the sinking helicopter and splashed around, trying to not get sucked down. Nanook dove under her and gave her a shove in the direction of shore. Or so he hoped. Their only light source sank, and once it died, they'd truly be in the dark.

A body brushed by him, a caribou—but not Dani—telling Nanook that Charlie had made it out. He couldn't see who else was in the vicinity. Kira and Arnie would be fine. As would Rook and Weaver. Hopefully Gertie, a musk ox, and Felicia, their snow fox, could swim to shore. Nanook could only handle one person per rescue, and he chose Dani.

Her spindly legs fluttered in the water, a water so frigid even he felt it. He bumped under her, which caused her to thrash in panic. To show her he meant to help and wasn't a predator looking to eat, he bobbed up alongside her, a faint bear face in the scarce visibility.

She bleated.

He rumbled and dove under again. He had no good way of holding her, not in their current shapes. Therefore, he did what he could to keep her afloat and heading in the direction of shore. They were within sight of it when she went completely limp. It led to him submerging and rising under her until she straddled his back sideways. He began paddling for land and had it in sight when a cross-current drew his attention.

There were a few possibilities of the source. Curious seals. Easy enough to scare off. A walrus, which could be trickier, given their weight and tusks. In this case, the culprit surfaced ahead of him, or the tip of its horn a least.

A narwhal.

People coined them the unicorns of the sea. They weren't that cute. They could stab and stun with their single tusk and weren't friendly one bit. Then again, polar bears were known to eat them. In his defense, they tasted delicious.

The narwhal passed under him again, taunting and acting out of the norm. Usually, their species would flee at the sight of a polar bear. This one, however, seemed to want something. Given their carnivore diet, he could only assume it saw Dancer as a delicious meal.

Not today.

He kept swimming, hoping to reach shallow water and lose the whale.

Didn't happen. The tip of its horn rose suddenly under him, stabbing at his belly. He threw himself sideways, so it grazed along his ribs instead of penetrating. However, in avoiding being impaled, he dropped Dancer, and she began to sink.

Shit. He headed under to grab her, his mouth grabbing her by a short horn and hauling her back to the surface. He'd no sooner cleared her head than the narwhal returned, the tunneling pressure of the water his only warning.

He released Dancer to whirl and clasp the horn as it neared. He grabbed hold and the narwhal didn't like it one bit. It shook its head, trying to dislodge him. As if Nanook had such a weak grip. His clawed hind feet dug into the whale's back, and he added his teeth to the horn, holding it tight. As he pulled on the protruding appendage, his paws braced, giving him the leverage needed to tear the bony protrusion free from the narwhal's head.

It thrashed, and he let go, moving away from the bloody water that would draw scavengers. He swam back towards where he'd last seen Dancer. Sunken again. He dove under and kicked, instinct more than anything guiding him to the sinking reindeer.

Once more, he got under her frame and used his body to lift, propelling upward, with her balanced on his back. He crested the sea and kicked hard for shore. Kept swimming until his feet touched the icy land.

He would have liked to rest. To collapse and relax for a moment after that ordeal. However, Dani had gone past the point of shivering. She wheezed weakly on the icy beach, hypothermia setting in.

Therefore, much as he'd like a break, he couldn't have one. Instead, he went to work building a shelter rather than go looking for survivors of the crash.

And when he couldn't exactly build a fire to keep her warm once it was done, he did the only thing he could think of with the shivering, wet reindeer. Draped her over his body like a blanket.

9

> Deer asleep on mountain high,
> Gently snoring, o'er the ice plains,
> And the mountain in reply,
> Growled out her nickname.

ONCE MORE, Dancer woke atop of a warm and snuggly bear. Naked, but not cold. Surprising since, last she recalled, she thought she'd die. The helicopter crash into the sea had left her convinced she'd drown as the intense cold water sapped her strength and vitality.

Somehow, she survived, and she'd wager she owed it all to the bear snoring underneath her.

She snuggled the fur on his chest and murmured, "Thanks for saving my life."

He huffed hotly.

"Going to assume that means 'you're welcome.'" She couldn't see anything around her, the darkness complete. She reached out a hand to see what she could feel and met a surface of ice. "You found us a cave."

He made a noise, and as her fingers kept questing, she found a seam, so she corrected her statement to, "You built us a shelter."

Growr.

"I'll take that as a yes." She sat up gingerly on the big furry body, pleased to see her head didn't bump the ceiling. "Where are we?" she murmured aloud, not expecting an answer, only he suddenly shifted.

Bear turned into man. A naked man whose taut belly she straddled. She splayed her hands on his chest to keep from falling over.

"We're at the North Pole," he murmured.

"We actually made it?" She couldn't help but sound surprised. "Where are the others?" She sensed no one else in this cocoon he'd made them.

"Don't know. Lost them when we crashed. How are you feeling?"

"Not bad, actually." She rolled her limbs to check them for soreness. "Seem to be intact. What happened after I blacked out?"

"I managed to get a hold of you and swam us to shore."

She arched a brow. "And the blood I scent is from…"

"A narwhal," he grumbled. "Blubbery jerk came at me while I was trying to keep you afloat."

"Jumping Jack in the box. I'm glad you're okay."

"Bah, would take more than a narwhal to bring me down. Besides, it did me a favor. Once I had the shelter built, it washed ashore. Hungry? I've got chunks of it to feed us both."

Her stomach gurgled. "I am a bit peckish."

"Can you get off me for a second so I can grab some?"

"Do I have to?" She sighed. "You're so nice and warm."

"You need to eat to keep up your strength."

He had a point. She slid from his warm—and very nicely muscled—belly to the cold floor of their shelter. Not as cold as it could have been, she realized. He'd spread the narwhal's skin over it. Moist and a bit spongy, but better than crouching on pure ice.

Another section of the skin hung over the door to their shelter. He tugged it aside, and the greenish lights of the aurora let her see a little bit while, at the same time, admitting a chilly draft that had her wrapping her arms around herself.

He pulled in two hunks of meat, handing her a section, while keeping one for himself.

Usually, she wouldn't eat raw in this state, but shifting meant no talking. It also meant she couldn't be dragged back into his warm lap, which he did after cursing. "You're shivering already."

She sat on his thighs and ate while ignoring the erection that poked under her. She was hungrier than expected and felt clearer-headed and stronger when done.

A noise of satisfaction escaped from Dancer as she finished, licking her fingertips. "I needed that. Thanks."

"You're welcome."

"Not just for the food but saving my life."

"Bah." He scoffed.

"I mean it. You could have let me sink and saved yourself."

"I'm not that kind of man."

"No, you're not," she agreed. "For a grumpy ice bear, you're actually nicer than you want people to know."

"Am not," he huffed.

"If you say so. Maybe I should have nicknamed you Pooh Bear instead of Nookie."

"Take that back," he growled.

"Why? I mean I think it's cute you're a big softie. Would you prefer Teddy?"

"I'm warning you, Dani." A low rumble from a predator that should have sent her fleeing but instead excited.

"I don't know why you're getting mad. Nothing wrong with being a nice guy."

"I am not nice."

"You are to me."

"I tried to toss you out the first time we met."

Her lips quirked. "But didn't because you're grumpy, not mean."

"I refused to help you."

"You had your reasons. But you're a good man. A great bear. And this might sound odd given all that's happened, but I'm glad we met."

"You are?" He didn't hide the surprise in his reply.

"Yes, I am, even if we failed our mission." Her lips turned down, not that he could see in the dark, but he caught the tone.

"Who says we've failed?"

"We're naked, without weapons or the reinforcements we brought."

"Not ideal," he admitted. "But that's not going to stop me from rescuing my girls."

"Of course we're going to try and free them. We have to make the attempt, but our chances of success were slim before. Now they're non-existent."

"Giving up already?"

"Being realistic."

"I thought everyone who worked for Santa was overly optimistic."

She snorted. "You're thinking of Cupid. She's annoying happy all the time."

"And you're not?"

"It's not that I'm unhappy. I have a good life. A great job."

"I hear a but."

"But ever feel like something's missing?" Not something she'd ever admitted out loud before.

"I know what you mean. I feel like a shit father when I get that way. I mean, my girls are my life. I love them so damned much, but sometimes I yearn for something more than making them breakfast and picking up their stuff."

"You're lonely like me."

"How can I be lonely with my two cubs?"

"Because it's not the same as a companion. Someone who understands grownup issues. Someone you can rely on. Someone to snuggle at night." She paused. "Someone to share intimacy with."

"I don't need a woman to complete me," he blustered.

"Then you're lucky. Me, I'd like to have someone to wake up to in the morning."

"Better hope they don't mind you smothering them like a blanket."

"Why, Nookie, is that a complaint? Would you prefer I slept with someone else?"

"No!" He shouted the word almost as if he were jealous.

Wishful thinking on her part. "So, Mr. Let's-go-invade-Santa's-Village, do you have a plan where we don't die the moment we try?"

"Not yet, but I'll think of something. I have to get my girls back. All the kids, for that matter."

"We'll need a ton of luck for that to happen."

"Anything is possible if you believe."

What she believed was that she might be falling for this enigma of a man. A man who would die before admitting defeat.

"I believed in Christmas miracles until this happened," she admitted.

"Who says we won't get one?"

"It's Christmas Eve."

"The perfect time to pull off an impossible feat."

She shook her head and sighed. "When did you become the positive one in this relationship?"

"Since I met a reindeer who wouldn't give up." He shifted her in his lap until she faced him in the darkness. "Don't let a few setbacks ruin your outlook on life."

"A few setbacks?" she snorted. "Have you forgotten what happened?"

"I haven't. And we survived. Seems to me like we're on a winning streak."

"And what's the prize if we do pull off the impossible?"

"Isn't saving the kids and Christmas enough?"

"Both are awesome, but I think I want something a little more selfish. Something just for me."

"And what does Dani want?"

She almost said "you," but settled for, "A kiss."

"From who?" asked the dense bear.

"You, Nookie."

"Oh." He sounded flummoxed. It lasted for a second, and then his lips were pressing against her. Stealing all thought. Making her heart pound and her horns throb.

When he was done rocking her world—and libido—he pulled back and smiled. "Let that be your incentive. Once we prevail, I'm going to kiss your other lips."

It took her a second to understand.

Then she blushed, flushed, and creamed herself.

He inhaled sharply.

"Damn, Dani. You sure know how to make a bear forget what's going on."

"Is that a bad thing?"

Before he could reply, a voice from outside startled.

"Ahoy, people inside the igloo."

"Stay here while I go see who it is."

She'd already recognized the speaker as Rook.

Despite the tight space, Nanook invited the naked

man in. Not that she caught more than a glimpse in the green light. Rook entered and took a spot opposite her, the dark of their shelter keeping her from seeing anything interesting. But that didn't stop Nanook from placing her in his lap, arm loosely around her. Staking his claim? A part of her kind of hoped so. She'd not known him long, but something about Nanook attracted her. To think he might be possessive or jealous warmed her insides like marshmallows in hot cocoa.

"Did you spot any of the others?" Nanook asked after Rook ate some of the narwhal meat.

"No, but a few things did wash up on shore. One of the kit bags. Some random bits of clothing."

"Grmph." Nanook grunted.

"What made those birds attack the chopper?" Rook asked.

Nanook shrugged, which proved interesting given they were both naked and skin to skin. "What made those walrus and wolverines decide to follow this Krampus?"

Dancer blurted out, "Is he like the Pied Piper?"

"The what?"

"It's a folk tale, not sure of its roots, but it's about a guy who plays an instrument and gets the rats to obey him."

"I know that story," Rook exclaimed. "Did you hear music playing?"

"Not that I recall," she admitted. "But he must be controlling his army somehow."

"Maybe he made them a deal," Nanook muttered.

"If they were shifters, I'd say yes, but these were animals."

"How can you be sure?" Rook questioned.

"Scent. The few that got close were of the wild variety. But if this Krampus managed to get them to obey, then why not birds?"

"You'd better hope he can't do that, else that means all the creatures out here might be ready to attack," Nanook warned.

Grawr. A bear bugle from outside had Nanook stiffening. "That's my sister." He gargled back, and soon a head poked through the flap, noticed their tight shelter, and shifted. Kira crawled in, followed by Arnie.

"Holy icicles, I am glad to see you," she exclaimed. "What a wild swim that was. We had to fight off some seals on our way to shore, which I've never encountered before."

"Narwhal for me," Nanook admitted.

"Are we all that's left?" Kira asked.

"Dunno. I've been holed up here making sure Dancer recovered from her polar plunge."

"Good idea building a big igloo. Once we saw it, we came straight over for a peek," Kira stated.

"Same," Rook added. "Else I might have kept wandering the beach."

As it turned out, the shelter Nanook built ended up drawing most of the survivors. Weaver found them next, by which time the shelter got very crowded and warm, warm enough with so many bodies they kept the flap open, leading to a bit of green light entering.

Then Benedict and Leroy stumbled onto them, the

pair of them having survived the crash by surfing an ice floe to shore. At their arrival, Nanook suggested some of them go scrounging for any supplies that might have washed ashore and to see if they could find the other missing members of their group. Missing not dead because no one wanted to think the worst.

Kira took the spot beside Dancer and leaned close to whisper, "So, are you and Nanook a couple?"

Dancer wished. "No."

"Are you sure? Because he's not touched a woman since Anjij left."

"He was just keeping me warm."

"Sure he was," drawled his sister.

"He was. He's a good man."

Kira snorted. "Not many would say that."

"Surely you would."

"Of course I would. He's my brother and a great father to his girls, but to other people? He's usually a bit of a dick."

"Oh, he's grumpy," Dancer agreed, "but deep down, he's a caring bear."

"You mean grouchy bear," snickered Weaver, who'd stayed behind to tend the wound on his foot. He'd encountered a crab while wading to shore.

Dancer took offense. "He saved my life."

"Whoa, wasn't trying to piss you off. I've just known him longer, and the guy you describe ain't the one I know."

A comment that oddly pleased her.

When the group returned, they'd managed an

eclectic haul that involved some soggy clothes and one knapsack, which Kira squealed upon seeing.

"Yay."

The reason soon became clear. She had packed a flint in that waterproof bag, which ended up being just the thing to light some narwhal blubber on fire. They hung the sodden garments around it and then had a meeting.

"So, we need a plan to get into the village and rescue the kids," Nanook started.

"With what? We lost the guns," Rook pointed out.

"We have no clothes," Weaver added.

"So, we go as our animals. They're better suited to this climate, anyhow," Nanook's reply.

"We'll need more than a few bears to take down this Krampus," Benedict stated. "I wish we'd have found at least a pistol or a rifle. I could have provided ground cover."

Which led to Dancer snapping her fingers. "What if I could get you some arms?"

"How?" asked Nanook. He'd not dragged her onto his lap since they had a warm fire, but he sat beside her.

"The QUEEF's hole."

Reaver coughed. "Er, what?"

"It's what they call the storage room for their weaponry because it's literally a hole in the ground. Given some of the ammo is explosive, and the gingerbread houses not exactly secure, Santa had the elves chisel out a chamber of ice to store it."

Nanook asked. "How do we get into QUEEF's hole?"

"Does it matter? It's in the village, which we can't enter without being noticed," Weaver argued.

Dancer shook her head. "Santa didn't want it inside the village in case of an incident. So, he has it by the training field instead."

"Surely the entrance is guarded," Weaver countered.

"Oh, I'm sure it is. The tunnel to it is under the barracks."

"I'm confused. How does that help us?" Weaver asked, while Nanook eyed her with curiosity.

She smiled. "Because, while they might be watching the true entrance, we'll be going in another way."

"There's a back door?" Nanook questioned.

"Not yet. But surely a guy who can build an igloo with his bear paws can create a new entrance in the ice."

10

On the day before Christmas, a reindeer
  gave to me,
A plan that might help with victory.

NO ONE HAD A BETTER IDEA, so despite the qualms about Dancer's plan to break into the armory, they went with her idea. They sent Leroy ahead to scout, his ability to fly making him their best spy.

Meanwhile, they bundled what they'd salvaged into a pack, and Dancer affixed it to Nanook's bearishly wide back—thank goodness Kira believed in using long straps—and then shifted to her reindeer shape. They trundled off, led by Dancer, who guided them by following the patterns she knew in the stars. By her estimate, they weren't too far from the village, only two miles. Two miles of open terrain and unknown threats.

Thankfully, she travelled with predators. Weaver and Rook roamed left, Kira and Artie took the right.

Their job? To hopefully prevent them from being ambushed while they dug their way into the armory.

An owlish Benedict chose to ride on Nanook's back, his sharp eyes scanning ahead.

As they neared the training field, Leroy returned with his feathers ruffled. Rather than all of them freezing to get his report, Dancer shifted. She might have been cold but for a furry bear coat wrapped around her, keeping her warm. Poor Leroy though. His skinny body shivered and his teeth chattered as he relayed what he'd seen.

"There's about six wolverines stationed in the training field. Several are hiding in the chimneys."

"What about the village itself?"

"It's got walrus ringing it every dozen or so yards. Big bastards too. About a dozen or so. I also saw wolverines inside that perimeter. Harder to give you an accurate count since they were constantly moving," Leroy recounted. "There's birds perched on Santa's house rooftop. Not a huge amount, although there's indication there used to be a lot more, as the snow on all the house tops is disturbed."

"Did you see any elves?"

Leroy shrugged. "Not out and about, but there appear to be some factories running, judging by the plumes coming up from their stacks. There's a pair of Yeti sitting outside Gingerbread Hall's main door and a walrus guarding the rear entrance."

Two Yeti. Yikes. "Did you see Krampus?"

He shook his head. "Nobody with horns or two legs, for that matter."

"Anything else?" she asked.

"I did see some of the reindeer. They appeared to be pulling a wagon full of crates from a factory to a big barn."

A relief to hear some had survived. "Any sign of the kids?"

"Nope. Nor of Santa. I tried dipping down to get a peek inside some windows, but some damned arctic terns came after me."

"Did they realize what you were?" she asked.

"Doubtful. They were simple-minded birds. Gentle usually, too, so them attacking was a surprise."

"Thanks for the intel."

"No problem. I'll head back to the sky and warn you if anything changes on the ground."

Leroy shifted and flapped off.

Dancer craned to look at her bearish protector. "You heard all that. How should we handle the wolverines in the field?"

He bared his teeth.

"Obviously you'll crunch them, but if they're in the chimneys, you'll have a hard time sneaking up on them. Not to mention, if one runs off to tattle about our presence, it could bring back more. We need to draw them out. Bait them with something innocuous so they don't think to warn anyone."

Benedict ruffled his feathers and cocked his head.

"While I appreciate the offer, I have a better idea." She stepped away from Nanook's warm embrace. "Be ready." With that said, she shifted into her reindeer and took off at a fast trot. Behind her, Nanook uttered a low rumbling growl.

He'd just caught on to what she meant by bait.

Wolverines loved fresh meat. Especially reindeer. She'd have to be fast and tricky if this was going to work.

Her hoofs clopped on the ice, kicking up puffs of snow as she neared the training field. The snowy roofs reminded her that tonight should have been the Christmas run. Could they free everyone in time to save it? The efficient elves had the gifts packed weeks ago, but Krampus might have tampered with the bag. Even if he hadn't, what if Santa was injured? Did they have anyone that could take his place? It had only ever happened once before when Santa fell ill and couldn't make the trip. With Santa incapacitated, everyone had pulled together, and Christmas happened, but not without some glitches. Boys getting dolls instead of trucks. Some good kids getting coal. Not ideal, but better than no Christmas at all.

As Dancer neared one of the fake chimneys, she put on a burst of speed, bolting past fast enough that the wolverine who sprang from it fell short. It hit the ground and scrambled to its feet with a snarl before giving chase.

Its sharp barks drew other wolverines from their hiding spots, eight as it turned out. Six in chimneys but two hid under the eaves of the roofs.

With them hot on her tail, she zigged and zagged. Even then it proved close as the rabid beasts converged, trying to trap her inside a noose of furious fur. Before it tightened, she ran for the closest slavering beast. It braced its front paws and snarled, ready to tear out her throat.

Dancer coiled her hindquarters and leaped. Soared right over the snapping menace in a beautiful arc before landing on the other side, still running, heading straight for the charging polar bear. Nanook to the rescue.

The wolverines, hot on her scent, didn't notice the new threat and followed in a rabid stream. She angled slightly to her left and ran past Nanook, who stuck out a paw and batted the first foe readying to lunge and bite at her hind leg. The wolverine yelped and hit the ground, injured.

The bear stomped it just as the other wolverines launched themselves at the furry polar threat. Nanook roared and stood, the wolverines hanging from him, their jaws clamped to his fur. While they were busy trying to chew on her Nookie, she ran and lowered her head. Her horns might be nubs in her human shape, but as a reindeer, they were three-tined and sharp-tipped. She gored the beast hanging off his ass, a perfect penetrating poke that made the wolverine squeal. She flicked her head and flung it away. Another went flying as Nanook grabbed it, chomped it—*crunch*—then tossed it aside.

One wolverine decided it had made a poor life choice and tried to flee, but a snowy owl hopped from a snowbank and landed on its back, digging in its talon while the mongrel yelped. A peck of its beak to the back of its neck severed its spine, and the wolverine went limp.

Meanwhile, Nanook was having a grand time playing with his attackers. Grabbing them with his claws and flinging them into the air, high enough they landed hard and didn't move again.

In short order, the fight was over and a naked Nanook glared at her and bellowed, "What were you thinking using yourself as bait?"

He deserved a reply, so she also shifted. "I was thinking you would protect me, duh." She rolled her eyes as she shivered in her nakedness. "Now, if you don't mind. It's cold. Yell at me later. Or better yet, give me the tongue-lashing I deserve." Said with an impish grin before she shifted back.

He stood there in shock. His cock also stood for another reason before he changed back into his bear—with a massive erection and fat tight furry balls.

A smug Dancer trotted ahead of him, head held high, and led him to the other side of the field, where, by her calculation, the armory should be situated underground.

She lowered her head to sniff, but her sense of smell couldn't discern where exactly to dig. She pawed at the ground and rolled her shoulders in a shrug.

Nanook eyed the surface before putting his nose down and giving the area a good sniff. Only after he'd gone around twice did he choose a spot to start digging. Snow and ice flew as he tunneled, the hole widening quickly. As it deepened, his upper body disappeared until only his ass remained visible.

Kira and Arnie lumbered into view, their fur a little ragged but unmarred by blood. The pair saw what Nanook did and joined him, both wiggling their asses as they dug and dug.

Dug a little too well since, suddenly, the ground underfoot collapsed, taking Dancer with it.

11

> Digging through the snow,
> A polar escapade.
> Down through ice they go,
> Smashing all the way.

NANOOK MISCALCULATED. A stress fracture in the roof of the hidden chamber suddenly cracked and spread too rapidly for him to warn. It all came down, a whoosh that dumped him, Kira, and Arnie in a rubble of ice.

Nanook emerged unscathed, as did the other bears, but the glimpse of a tufted tail buried under the cold debris put him in a panic.

Dani!

She didn't appear to be moving. Nanook began grabbing and flinging the chunks in his way, tossing them out of the hole as he made his way to her.

Being as gentle as he could be, Nanook plucked Dani from the wreck. Her head lolled limply, but she breathed. He hugged her to his chest and rocked her.

Sorry. So sorry. He should have had her standing much farther back.

His sister, who'd swapped into her human form, cleared her throat. "If you keep squeezing her, you'll crush something."

He replied with a bear glare.

"She's fine," Kira insisted. "Just knocked out for the moment."

Just? He growled.

The body in his arms shifted from reindeer to human and stirred. Dani uttered a slurred, "Did I crash again?"

He nosed her, and she giggled. "That's cold." Her lashes fluttered. "Hello, Nookie. Thanks for coming to my rescue again."

Grawr.

"Yes, you are a handsome hero," she murmured. Her lips curved. "Although, right now, I can't help but think we look like that Bugs Bunny cartoon."

When his nose scrunched in confusion, Kira sang, "I will hug her and pet her and squeeze her…"

"Just don't call me George," Dani said with a laugh. "You can put me down now."

He held on to her instead.

Kira rummaged in the pack on his back and removed two blankets. She handed one to Dancer. "Let's try and not freeze off our tits while we take a poke around."

Dancer wrapped it around herself, but her bare feet concerned Nanook. He went on his four paws and wiggled.

"What's he doing?" Dancer asked.

Kira understood. "He's telling you to get on his back." She then cast a look at her husband. "Because someone is a gentleman who doesn't want his woman's feet to get cold."

Arnie chuffed.

"Did you just call me too fat to sit on your back?" Kira asked with an arched brow.

Her husband lay down in front of her in invitation, but Kira patted him. "Thanks for offering, but we both know I'd totally mess with your sciatica."

Dancer hugged Nanook's bulky body as he gingerly stepped through the wreckage. A wreckage that lacked something.

"I don't see any weapons," she stated.

"I noticed the same thing." Kira bent and craned for a peek under a large, slanted slab of ice. "The shelves are all empty."

"Krampus must have raided it when he took over the village. We came here for nothing." Dani sounded disappointed.

However, Nanook gave a little shake. Dani grabbed the fur at his neck and exclaimed, "Whoa, big fellow."

"I think my brother is trying to convey something."

"What?"

Kira frowned. "I'm not sure."

Nanook stepped over the debris and made his way across the chamber open to the sky. It took nosing a few fallen pieces of ice for his sister to clue in.

"He's looking for the tunnel."

"The one that leads into the village," Dancer

exclaimed. "We could totally use it to enter undetected. Only, won't it be guarded at the other end?"

He nodded then gave a ferocious growl.

"Yes, you could eat them, but you'd have to do so quickly and quietly so they don't give warning we've infiltrated," Dani stated.

"A diversion might help in that respect," Kira mused aloud. "Rook and Weaver could perhaps cause some trouble on the perimeter. Add in Leroy as well and a slight commotion inside might not be noticed."

"The tunnel exits into the barracks. If Krampus has its troops stationed in there, we'll be hard-pressed to get past them."

"Wolverines inside a building? Seems unlikely." Kira sounded skeptical. "A walrus, however…"

"Would have a tough time fitting through the door," Dancer stated. "While they can accommodate a human, a walrus is much wider."

Nanook huffed, and Kira snickered. "I think he just said his ass is just as big."

He bared his teeth, but his sister laughed.

"Even if we assume the interior has only minimal threat, getting to Gingerbread Hall means crossing Holiday Square. The Yeti will spot us."

"Assuming Krampus is in the hall," Kira reminded. "Seems more likely to me that a despot would want the luxury of Santa's house to rule from."

"Leroy did say the birds were perched on its roof," Dani murmured. "Santa's house might make the better option. Not only is it closer to the barracks, but I know for a fact he's got his own set of tunnels, including one that goes right to Gingerbread Hall."

"Guess that settles it then. We're going to visit Santa," Kira chirped.

"Even though it's close, we still have to expose ourselves getting from the barracks to it."

"Which is where a diversion would come in handy. Something to draw the enemy out of the area, giving us an opening to sneak to our objective."

"I'm a little skeptical at how well a polar bear can sneak," Dani's dry reply.

"Ask my kids. I can be stealthy as heck. One of my joys of motherhood is scaring the piss out of them." Kira grinned.

"Who's going to tell Rook, Weaver, and Leroy about the plan?"

Benedict had to be briefed too. While Nanook cleared space in the passage, she told him the plan. The snow owl hung his head. Most likely feeling left out since he couldn't fly.

But Dani had an idea for him. "The armory isn't the only place we had weapons stored. While not as deadly, the barracks will have some hot cocoa guns and candy cane slingers."

The owl blinked at her.

"I know they're not as efficient as a rifle, but better than nothing, right?"

Benedict gave her a nod.

Maybe they could still make this work. Nanook had his doubts. He'd really counted on them being able to sharpshoot the biggest threats. A Yeti was no easy thing to fight. And a pair of them? Things would get ugly.

For the Yeti and anyone else in his path.

Losing wasn't an option. His girls needed their Dada to save them.

The tunnel appeared empty, but he still scented those who'd had passed through. Elves. And only elves.

He could see only two reasons for that. Either they were mounting a counterattack or they were in cahoots with Krampus.

If the latter, no one would say shit when he ate them.

He just hoped they didn't all taste like peppermint. Couldn't stand the smell or taste since that fateful day. He did, however, like the sweet flavor of Dani's lips. The kiss had been impromptu, but he didn't regret it. Humans might take weeks, months, years to know what they wanted in a mate. Nanook, however, tended to be more decisive. And he'd decided in the last few hours he wanted Dani.

All the more reason to be successful.

With the tunnel cleared, time to act. Arnie had found and briefed Weaver and Rook. In a slight change, the three polar bears would work as a team to provide the distraction, along with Leroy. Kira and Benedict would stay with Nanook and Dani.

They set off, Nanook taking the lead, with Benedict perched on his back. Dani shifted and trotted behind, while Kira brought up the tail.

The tunnel proved eerily silent, the usual music that played in the village absent, but their path remained lit by globes inset in the walls. They encountered no guards during their trek, which he found odd. Then again, would this Krampus have expected them to literally burrow their way in?

The end of the tunnel ended in stairs and still no guard. As they climbed the icy steps to the hatch, everyone kept very quiet. Nanook pressed his head against the closed hatch to listen. Heard nothing. He used his shoulders and back to shove, flinging it open quickly and then popping out, ready to attack.

Only to find himself surrounded, hot cocoa guns pointed at his head and a squeaky voice saying, "Halt or we'll shoot."

12

Jingle bells,
Elves always smell,
Of candy and chocolate.

DANCER HEARD the squeaky threat and shifted as she pounded up the steps and threw herself in front of Nanook.

"Don't shoot!" she yelled to the ragged gang of elves holding the weapons.

Wearing a hat that had lost its bell, Ding-a-ling blinked at her. "Dancer?"

"Hey, Ding-a-ling."

"How did you get here? Everyone thought you died in the initial assault."

She shook her head. "I managed to escape and brought back help."

Ding-a-ling grinned. "We're saved. I can't believe you managed to get FUCDD." FUCDD being the Furry

United Coalition Department of Defense. Their military branch.

"Not exactly," she stated. "A storm blew me off course, and I ended up with the FARTZ, who currently have no way of getting in touch with any FUCs."

"Then who's that?" Ding-a-ling pointed to Nanook, who chose that moment to block her girly bits from view and glare.

"That's Nanook, who is a retired FUCDD. The owl is Benedict, also military, and that other bear is Kira, Nanook's sister."

The elf's smile fell. "You brought three people? That's not even enough to handle the Yeti, unless you brought fruitcake."

"We're just part of the rescue team," she admitted as she chewed her lip. Perhaps mentioning the fact they were so few could wait. "How is it you're here in the barracks? I figured Krampus would have everyone sequestered in Gingerbread Hall."

"Only the old and the very young. They're holding them hostage to ensure good behaviour while we work."

"Krampus is making toys?" She couldn't hide her surprise.

"No. Krampus is converting the toy factories to make weapons like guns and bombs. Whereas the Candy Factory is now concocting some kind of potion."

Her eyes widened. "What's Krampus planning?"

Ding-a-ling shook his head. "No idea but it can't be good."

At Nanook's grumble, she quickly asked, "Have you seen some children? They would have arrived yesterday. Krampus kidnapped them from the folks in FARTZ."

A female named Hollybell stepped forward. "I saw them. They're with the other kids in the hall."

"Unharmed?"

"As far as we can tell."

Kira, who'd been quiet until now, pointed to the gun. "Are you the ones who emptied the armory of weapons?"

"That would be Krampus. Confiscated every weapon in the village. This"—Ding-a-ling waved the pistol—"was part of my personal stash."

"You said the adults were working, yet you're here," Dancer pointed out.

"Krampus has no idea how many of us there are. Some of the other elves covered for us so we could slip away in the hopes we could figure out a way to free the rest. Alas, so long as the old and young'uns are prisoner, we dare not do much."

"We need to cut the head off the puppet master," Dani stated. "Get rid of Krampus, then the wolverines and other creatures being controlled should revert back to normal." AKA trying to eat them because they were hungry and not because someone told them to.

"That won't be easy. He's holed up in Santa's house," Hollybell informed.

"He's got a walrus just inside the front door, a big mean one," stated another elf whom she didn't know by name.

"Then I guess we'll have to find another way in."

Nanook grumbled.

"Yes, I know you can take a walrus, but we're looking for the element of surprise, remember?" She glanced at Ding-a-ling. "How else can we get inside?"

"The windows are shatterproof," the elf mused aloud. "And the tunnel to the hall would obviously require you getting past the Yeti."

It was Kira who said, "What about the chimney?"

Again, Nanook made a noise.

Kira snorted. "Obviously you won't fit. Neither of us would, but..." Her gaze slewed to Dancer and Benedict.

Nanook shifted abruptly to state, "No fucking way."

"Don't be so quick to say no," Dancer interjected. "You were the one who said if we take the head of the insurgent out, we win. If we can get inside, then Benedict just needs to shoot Krampus."

"Not we. Bennie doesn't need you to do his job," he growled.

"But he could use the support," she retorted. "Not to mention, I know how to get into Santa's personal workshop."

"It's too dangerous."

"More dangerous than escaping some wolverines, flying in a storm across the sea, crashing, running into a polar bear, taking a helicopter back across the sea, crashing again and almost freezing to death?"

He growled, but Dancer held her ground. "This mission is dangerous for everyone, but we don't have a choice. Krampus has to die."

"You think this fucker is going to stand still while you shoot? There could be more guards inside we don't know about."

"Which is why you and I will go knocking at the door," Kira stated. "While we tussle with the walrus and cause a distraction, Benedict and Dancer slip in, handle the threat. If this Krampus is controlling the animals, then, with its death, they should disperse and we can go grab our kids."

"What if there's more than a walrus inside?" Nanook argued.

"Then I will do my best to not get killed." Bravest thing Dancer ever said aloud.

Kira's head swivelled as sharp yips and grunts of the enemy sounded. "We don't have time to argue. Seems like the boys are giving us the distraction we asked for." She glanced at Nanook. "I know you don't like this plan, but we don't have a choice. So, let's give her and Benedict the best shot at success by reducing those in their way. So, brother, shall we go hunt us some walrus? You know I have a recipe for the meat."

Nanook grabbed Dancer rather than replying, lifting her so they were eye to eye. "If you die, I will be very angry."

"As opposed to…"

He growled.

She grinned. "Don't worry, Nookie. I plan to survive. After all, someone owes me a kiss. Now, shall we go save Christmas?"

"Yeah!" The ragged band of elves cheered.

"We need to move quick. Ding-a-ling, I need a

weapon for Benedict. And clothes." Because she wasn't climbing onto Santa's roof naked.

The elves yanked stuff from the lockers. She and Benedict dressed quickly before taking the weapons handed to them. No one made any comment on how ridiculous they looked, the leggings barely reaching their knees and skintight, the tunics more like belly tops. Thankfully, everything, including the slippers, could stretch. The material was accommodating, if bright.

"Let's do this," she huffed, her heart racing with fear and adrenaline.

Nanook, back in his bear shape, gave her a long look before charging out of the barracks, roaring, Kira on his heels.

The elves surprisingly followed, singing of course. "Oh, come all ye faithful, elves will be triumphant!"

Dancer glanced at Benedict. "Ready?"

"No, but we're going anyhow."

They exited to an insane amount of noise, the raucous elves yodeling, the bears growling, and from in between the houses, the enemy came. Not many, thanks to Arnie, Rook, and Weaver having drawn some of them out of the village.

Nanook ignored the wolverines racing for him and headed left for Santa's house, the only one built of stone. Only a single story, it sprawled, the interior large, as it accommodated both his living quarters and his original workshop before he expanded.

While Nanook charged for the front door, Kira whirled to watch his back as the howling wolverines converged. The elves lined up on either side of Kira, holding up their candy cane slingers, which they began firing at the handful of wolverines racing for them.

Dancer glanced at Benedict, looking as ridiculous as her in the very tight elf clothing. "We can climb the porch to get to the roof." The railing was easy enough to get on top of. She'd hoped the walrus would emerge from the house to fight Nanook, but the door remained shut. Not for long, she'd wager, with the way Nanook kept barreling into it.

Across the square, she noticed the Yeti watching and yet not moving from their post. Not interested in engaging, or were they being coerced to stay there? Whatever the reason, it meant one less threat to deal with.

The railing proved slick, but Dancer managed to climb onto the porch roof and then turned to give Benedict a hand. His bum arm had less strength than his good one, but he managed on his own, grunting with effort.

As they stood to traverse to the rooftop, the Yeti suddenly visibly shook and stood from their post.

"Uh-oh," she muttered.

"Looks like Krampus gave them new orders," Benedict stated. "We better move fast."

The fresh snow made the tiles slick, and they had to step carefully to reach the chimney, which then led to a new dilemma. The smoke rising from it indicated a fire burned.

Dancer grimaced. "Guess we're singing our feet." She glanced at her slipper-covered toes.

"Not necessarily. Help me." Benedict reached down

DANCER AND THE ICE BEAR

and scooped some white stuff and dropped it down the chimney.

Duh. "Good idea." She joined him in dumping snow, with thick black smoke being their sizzling reward.

It stung the lungs and eyes. Benedict grimaced. "And to think I gave up drinking so I could do this." He grumbled, but he still climbed over the lip first and dropped down. Only a dozen feet or so, but Dancer chose to brace herself inside the chimney and went down more slowly. She emerged from the smoldering damp hearth to find Benedict in Santa's kitchen. A quiet place since the last Mrs. Claus died. Poor Santa. He'd had a few wives since the original Mrs. Claus, but whatever sustained him did not extend to his spouses and made him unable to have children.

The kitchen table held a mess of food, plates with remnants, containers opened and food inside partially eaten, dishes piled in the sink.

Benedict put a finger to his lips, as if that were necessary.

They tiptoed from the kitchen to the hall and held their breaths, as they could see the front door and the large walrus blocking it. The beast never noticed the intruders, too busy barking at the bears that came knocking. When those ferocious ice bears splintered the door, the chunky threat went humping outside.

With it gone, some of her tension eased. Benedict, though, remained stiff and alert.

The hallway had a few options. Washroom right across from the kitchen, the door wide open so they could see no one was inside. At the rear end of the hall was the bedroom, which took only a moment to check out, as its door also remained ajar. The big bed within had its covers rumpled but no one in it laying their head on a pillow dreaming of sugar plums.

The next room had no door, just an open arch, and Benedict peeked around the edge before he slid into the parlor with its coal-burning stove. A cozy space with books and a television from the seventies set in a big wooden frame.

He glanced at her and mouthed, "Where next?"

She sidled close and whispered, "Santa's old workshop." While the big man no longer needed to make toys, he still found a need for a private workspace.

Benedict glanced around the parlor with a frown. "Where's the door?" he hissed.

"Hidden." While Santa didn't believe in having locks in the village, he did keep his workshop secured. Most likely because it held the vault with his bible of Good and Naughty Children, as well as the dust he made. Flying powder, sleeping tonics, and she'd even heard rumors he fabricated other things inside.

Only a few knew how to enter. Technically, Dancer wasn't one of the privileged, except she'd happened to overhear drunken Rudolph boasting one day.

"Yeah, me and the big guy are close. He even gave me the combo to get into his secret room." Rudolph had been trying to impress some woman at the time.

Dancer, while knowing she shouldn't, had stayed to listen.

"He doesn't use a key?" the woman questioned.

"Nah. It's a puzzle lock based on the Twelve Days of Christmas. Only, the correct symbols don't match the verses."

"What do you mean?"

"Well, for example, the partridge in a pear tree? If you press that icon, a trap door opens. The actual correct one to push is the cat in the oak one."

"A cat?"

"Santa went with the things he liked more."

Rudolph had gone through them, one by one, although Dancer had wandered off around eight, as in between his telling, she'd heard the moist lip-smacking as they smooched. Given her crush on the famous reindeer, she'd not wanted to hear the next more carnal act to come.

But she remembered enough to feel somewhat confident until she stood in front of the wall carved with all kinds of images. The twelve ones for the regular poem, but dozens of others. A goat in a tree. Two turtle doves, but there were also a pair of flamingoes and elephants. The latter being the correct tile.

She pressed the cat in the tree, then the duo of elephants. The first eight she had no problem because, as soon as she saw the image, she remembered Rudolph's boasting, but on the ninth, she ran into issues.

"What's wrong?" Benedict hissed.

"I didn't hear the last four," she admitted.

"So, we're guessing now?" he asked, glancing at the wall.

"We know nine isn't the ladies dancing. What other nines are there?" She eyed the wall.

"There's nine chickens pecking," he pointed out.

She frowned. "Santa hates chicken. Says it reminds him of turkey, which he's not fond of." With that said, she pressed on the nine giraffes.

"What happens if you choose wrong?"

She glanced at her feet. "We end up in a pit."

Benedict's eyes widened, and he took a step back.

She perused the wall for the tens next. Ten leaping lords could be frogs or sheep. Santa loved his woolly jammies.

Click.

The floor didn't move.

Eleven was the fish dancing in the waves.

Which left twelve.

Not the twelve drummers. She glanced between the other two options. Twelve Christmas stars around a moon or twelve presents under a tree. Both seemed apt.

She frowned.

"Can't choose?"

"Neither seem right," she murmured.

"It's a fifty-fifty pick, and we need to get this done." Benedict kept glancing over his shoulder.

The sounds of fighting continued, but more surprising, Krampus didn't emerge from the secret room. Even if Krampus weren't inside, they needed access to the tunnel to reach the hall, to the Yeti.

She pursed her lips as she eyed the wall, wondering if she'd missed something. Her gaze went to the one tile that didn't match the rest. A portrait of Santa's first wife, smack-dab in the middle.

Before she could second-guess herself, she pressed it.

Click.

The door opened, and her jaw dropped at what she saw beyond.

13

Dashing into danger,
A one-bear polar menace.
Growling as he renders,
Smashingly overzealous.

NANOOK HEAD-BUTTED the massive walrus in the gut, shoving it back. The very chunky beast had emerged from the splintered doorway of Santa's house and humped its girth to attack. Some folks assumed a walrus on land would be slow and ineffectual.

Wrong.

Walrus were tough bastards, which meant Nanook had to be careful. He also had to pay attention. Thankfully, Kira and the elves handled the wolverine that kept trying to jump on his back, leaving him to face off against the brute.

The big wally barked at him, and Nanook snapped right back before lunging, but the wily beast proved fast and managed to avoid his chomping teeth.

Nanook crouched and watched the big beast as it swayed on the porch, honking, calling its friends. A herd of them would be trouble.

Time to end this fight.

He stood and went in with slashing claws. The walrus tried to stab him with its tusks, but a clenched paw to the face knocked its head sideways, and then Nanook was on top of the brute, tearing and slashing, ribboning, until it stopped moving.

Before Nanook could enter the house, the Yeti bugled. A glance showed them lumbering in their direction.

Not good. Polar bears had few true predators, but the abominable snow creatures? They ranked at the top.

A glance at his sister showed her standing and cracking her paws, getting ready. She bared her teeth in a ferocious polar version of a grin. He flanked her, the pair of them facing off against the mighty hairy Yeti stomping their way.

Ping. Ping. Candy canes began bouncing off the foreheads of the threat, tiny striped missiles that did nothing to slow their advance. But at least the elves tried.

Nanook had braced himself, readying to charge, when suddenly a bomb dropped from the sky.

Not a bomb, a fruitcake, delivered by none other than Leroy, who did an about-turn and flapped to a rooftop, where some elves waited with more.

The Yeti paused, and one of them scooped the cake. The other smacked it out of its hands. The first Yeti bellowed and threw itself on its companion. To

Nanook's surprise—and glee—the abominables began fighting with each other.

It didn't last long, with the first one drawing blood, which apparently was a sign to stop. The loser pouted, great big lower lip jutting, showing off its saber teeth. It resumed its march for Nanook and gang, while its companion ate the fruitcake.

Leroy dropped another loaf.

The second Yeti stamped its feet and snatched it, popping it into its mouth. The lure of the fruitcake stronger than the one to attack.

Ding-a-ling shouted, "We've got these abominables covered. Get inside and rescue Santa."

Nanook trundled into the house, his nose picking up a myriad of scents. Elf, not surprising. Santa, of course. Walrus, nasty. And polar bear.

He frowned, mostly because there was something familiar and, at the same time, off about the polar bear scent lingering inside. But he ignored it in favor of Dancer's aroma. He followed his nose into a living room where a section of wall gaped open and beyond...

He shifted to mutter, "What in the ever-snowing blizzard is going on here?"

With just a quick glance, he took in the scene. A long workbench of weathered wood covered in glass beakers and Bunsen burners, the array of them linked by tubing, through which flowed fluids of varying colors. He took in the massive safe in a corner with its door open and Santa's precious bible askew, lying on the floor. But the most perturbing sight of all?

Santa, spread eagle on a rack, with bindings around

his torso, wrists, legs. Even his neck had a strap. He appeared unconscious, his eyes shut, his breathing labored. The big fellow pale of countenance, most likely because of the IVs in both his arms pumping out his blood, which sparkled. Despite his desperation to find Dancer, he eyed the contraption hooked to Santa. He knew enough about them to figure out how to turn off the valve.

As Nanook stopped the flow, Santa opened a single bloodshot eye and peered blearily at him. "Thank the sugar plums you're here."

"What's going on?" Because, while he'd expected to find the big man captive, to see him ignobly drained baffled.

"Bad things," Santa muttered, his one eye fluttering shut.

"Don't pass out on me yet," Nanook grumbled. "Where's Dancer and Benedict?"

Santa kept his eyes closed as he murmured, "They went into the tunnel after Krampus and—"

Nanook had heard enough. "Sorry to leave, but I have to help them." The hole in the floor, with its hatch folded over, had to be where they'd gone. As he prepared to jump down, Santa gasped.

"Wait. There's things you have to know before you go rushing in."

He paused on the edge of the hole. "Like what?"

"Free me while I tell you."

The delay chafed. However, he'd always heard of how Santa was a mighty combatant. So mighty he'd been captured. Still, only those who wanted to be mounted as trophies rushed into bad situations without all the intel.

Nanook returned to the rack and began to unbuckle the restraints. "What happened to you?"

"I was fooled. Someone who left a while ago returned, begging for a second chance. I should have known better. Should have seen the naughty in their heart. Alas, adults are much harder to read than children. I let them into my home for a chat, and they drugged my tea. I woke, bound and impotent, my village taken hostage."

"Must have been some pretty good shit if it managed to take you down," he remarked as he bent to do the ankles, chafing at the delay. The bindings weren't simple leather he noticed. They appeared coated with something that left an unpleasant residue.

"The world today is capable of so much. A pity that those with bad intentions sometimes are the best innovators."

"Isn't that the truth," Nanook murmured. He understood because, in the military, he'd seen the weapons being developed. Each more horrible than the last.

Once he'd freed Santa's arms and legs, Nanook readied to go after Dancer.

"Before you leave, you should know Krampus isn't the real threat."

Once more he paused on the edge of the tunnel's hatch. "Then who is?"

Before Santa could reply, Nanook heard distant screaming, echoing up the tunnel. He jumped into the hole and, as he began running, heard Santa faintly call out after him. "Beware the past that returns to taunt you."

Cryptic shit. Why couldn't people ever give straight answers?

Nanook remained a naked man as he ran through the tunnel, hearing the screams, high-pitched like that of elves—or children.

The hatch at the far end of the corridor gaped wide open, and he emerged into an office, the big desk taking up the center obviously Santa's. Bookshelves lined the walls and held toys, the hand-carved type that he suspected Santa had designed himself. The door to the room remained ajar, and when he pushed through it, he found an unbelievable sight.

The most surprising thing? Not the giant elf with leathery skin wearing Santa's pants and coat. A red hat with a pompom hung off one curving horn. Nor was the surprising sight that of elves and kidnapped children, huddled crying against a wall. The thing that froze him in place? The sight of his girls in the grips of none other than their mother.

"Anjij?" He blinked, but she didn't disappear, looking paler than before but recognizable. How had he not known she'd returned to the North Pole? Why hadn't she contacted him? Or tried to see the girls?

His shock had him frozen in place until he heard a familiar voice.

"It's over, Jingles!" Dancer yelled bravely, facing off against the monster, which snarled.

"Obey me, reindeer. I am Santa," Jingles bellowed,

beating his leathery gray chest, the coat he wore gaping open.

"Ha, as if you could ever think to take his place," Dancer taunted, making Nanook wonder why she made the wannabe Krampus mad until he saw Benedict taking aim with his hot cocoa shooter.

Nanook knew before Benedict fired it would fail.

Splat.

The hot liquid with melting marshmallows hit Krampus in the face and dribbled. The monstrous elf licked its lips. "Yum. More." He opened his mouth wide and smirked.

"Crush them," Anjij yelled. "Crush those who would stand in the path of your greatness, oh mighty Krampus."

In that moment, Nanook understood—even as he could scarcely believe—Anjij was a part of the coup. Santa's parting remark made sense now.

Worse than that realization? She held his girls, clinging tight to their hands despite the fact they pulled to try and get away. His poor cubs wore a frightened look until they saw their Dada.

Siku spotted him first and stopped struggling. She smiled, and her lips moved, which led to Sesi stilling as well. Both his girls stared at him with all the confidence children could have in their parent.

Anjij noticed their distraction, and her full lips pulled into a scowl. "Your father can't save you. No one can. Get him, Krampus," she yelled. "Smash the bear who wants to keep us apart."

Krampus turned his gaze from a frustrated Benedict with his hot cocoa gun and fixed it on Nanook.

Time to bear out.

Nanook fluffed out, swapping to fur with a roar that Krampus met. He charged across the floor, noting how Benedict tugged Dancer out of the way.

In his transformed state, Jingles now loomed as tall as Nanook when he stood on his hind paws. At least the elf who'd ruined his life would be able to put up a fight —a failed one, as Nanook would take his life.

Nanook slammed into the mutant elf, who, to his surprise, didn't topple. Jingles grunted and held against Nanook's shoving force, which dropped his jaw wide open. Nanook uttered a grunt and heaved, grappling with the monster's unexpected strength. In a brute contest of force, they appeared evenly matched. Good thing Nanook knew some tricks. He slid a hind paw between Jingles' legs and hooked his ankle, throwing Jingles off balance. The elf hit the floor hard, with Nanook on top, but he didn't keep his position long. Jingles shoved and managed to fling Nanook away.

Suddenly airborne, Nanook couldn't do much but brace before he hit the floor. Nanook shook his head before standing to brace for the next run. Jingles also rose to his feet and uttered a strange bugling cry.

"You've injured me," the mutant elf screamed, whining about the tiny scratch on his cheek that bled a thick and strange green-colored ooze.

Nanook raced for Jingles just as Dancer yelled, "Holy shiny tinsel. He's getting bigger."

Indeed, the elf suddenly expanded, popping seams

on its garments, revealing even more of its mottled gray chest, the skin on it taut, so taut Nanook could see the outline of every bone. The face turned gaunt as flesh stretched to accommodate the new size.

Jingles thumped his chest and roared. "Ho. Ho. Ho." With his longer reach, Jingles swung and batted at Nanook, sending him rolling, the force behind the blow impressive.

As he rose once more to four paws, he heard his ex-wife cackle. "Make him bleed again, you big dumb oaf. Injuries only make Krampus stronger!"

The revelation surely couldn't be true. It made no sense.

Dancer reacted by hollering, "Liar! You don't want Nanook attacking because you're scared your plot to ruin Christmas is about to go up in hollyberry smoke."

"Why would I lie?" Anjij stated with a smirk. "Did you not notice my peppermint lover is now bigger than a Yeti? Every time he bleeds, he grows, his new special trait courtesy of a recipe left behind by a certain Mastermind, may the good genius rest in peace."

The name sent a shockwave through the shifters present. Everyone in their world knew that Mastermind had been behind horrible experiments on their kind. Taking innocent furries and other shapeshifters and making them into monsters.

"You won't succeed in your plot," Dancer insisted. "Good always prevails over evil."

"Does it? Because, from where I stand, it looks like I've already won," an overly confident Anjij stated.

Indeed, the situation didn't look good. Benedict,

impotent without a proper gun. Dancer brave but also without a weapon. Nanook might be the mightiest ice bear around, but even he found the foe he faced daunting.

Krampus grinned. "Ho. Ho. Ho. Who wants to sit on my lap?" With that, he bent down and reached for Dancer. She moved quickly out of the way, however, didn't flee to safety, instead remaining in the danger zone around the monster.

Nanook roared and rushed Krampus, staying on all his paws and lowering his head to ram. He might as well have struck a mountain for all the good it did. He hit Krampus just above the knee to no avail—unless a possible concussion counted.

Stunned at the impact, he couldn't avoid the swipe that sent him flying. He rolled and tumbled, coming to a stop at the feet of an older female elf.

She eyed him sadly. "Never thought I'd see Christmas end at the hands of a bad elf. Thanks at least for trying."

As if he'd give up.

Nanook rose and glanced at Krampus to see him swiping at a prancing Dancer. She'd shifted and, despite the snug tights and shirt that hadn't shredded, darted to and fro, teasing the monster, which made no sense until he saw Benedict climbing to the balcony behind Krampus with a spindle in hand. A broken chair had provided his friend with a sharp stake.

Benedict would only get one chance to stab. Nanook lumbered over to join Dancer in distracting Krampus, standing on his hind legs and roaring.

Jingles cackled. "Puny little teddy. Guess who's bigger now."

"Not you," Benedict yelled. "You're the peppermint scuzz your mom should have swallowed."

At the insult, Jingles whirled, only to shriek as a leaping Benedict shoved the stake through his chest before dropping to the floor.

Everyone held their breath as Jingles grabbed at the sliver of wood embedded in its flesh, right where his heart should be. The giant elf wailed, "Argh. I'm stabbed. Oh no. Oh… you idiots." The voice deepened, and to everyone's horror, the monster grew some more.

Benedict had missed its heart, if it even had one.

With the new bloody injury, Krampus grew so much his horns butted into the ceiling and, with a toss of his head, smashed through the roof, sending parts of it tumbling.

Everyone ran to get away from the falling debris. Dancer skirted past him, heading for the protection of the outer walls, where the elves huddled. Nanook stood behind her and used his body as a shield as parts of the building came down.

Crash.

"Bwahahaha." Jingles smashed through the hall and stomped outside, yelling, "Forget being Santa. I am Krampus. Emperor of the world."

"Not diddly-snickerdoodle likely," bellowed a deep voice.

It took an elf murmuring, "Santa!" for them to raise their heads and look to the sky through the ruined roof.

Overhead, illuminated by the green lights of the Aurora Borealis, appeared a figure on a reindeer.

Make that a caribou, because Charlie would have been insulted to be called otherwise. Yes, Charlie. No mistaking the grizzled old pilot who'd survived the crash after all, who now ran on air, carrying the big man.

"We're saved!" cheered the elves.

Nanook wasn't the only one to race through the rubble to get outside and watch the unfolding battle.

A Kong-sized Krampus stood in the middle of Holiday Square, scowling. "I knew we should have killed you. But, no, Anjij said, we need Santa, even though I said, 'no, my little pot of crème de menthe, we don't, because you have me.' I warned her you were tricky."

"Jingles, you've been a bad, bad elf," Santa stated in a voice that carried as he sat atop Charlie, who did circles overhead. "For your crimes, you are permanently on the naughty list and banned from the North Pole." The big man extended his red and white glowing striped sword, a sword Nanook thought was only legend.

"You and your rules. Blech." Jingles raspberried his tongue. "Elves are tired of listening to a fat human."

"No, we're not," squeaked an elf. Others watching on the outskirts murmured in agreement.

"Silence. You don't know what's good for you, but I do," Krampus declared. "Under my rule, we shall own the world. Humans will work for us."

"Have you seen their shoddy products? No thanks," shouted another elf.

"Give up now, Jingles, or face the consequences," Santa shouted.

"Never!" Jingles swung a massive fist, and Charlie had to dive to avoid getting swatted from the sky.

Everyone on the ground "oooh-ed" as Santa held on. How? Nanook couldn't have said. A man his size should have fallen if gravity applied.

Jingles kept swinging, preventing Santa from getting close. A distraction was needed. Just as Nanook prepared to provide it, a tiny fluffy form bolted from between two buildings. An arctic fox—Felicia! She had survived the helicopter crash and appeared in fine fox form. Fast as a child stealing a cookie, she darted between Jingles' legs, avoiding the stomping feet. To add to Nanook's astonishment, Benedict came charging, seated atop a musk ox—Gertie, in all her snorting ire. She bull-rushed Jingles, and Nanook had to wonder at the plan until he saw Benedict pull back a slingshot and let loose. Just a candy cane, but fired hard at Jingles' groin.

The tiny sting shouldn't have been a big deal, but the elf screamed. "My peppermint chocolate balls. Argh, you nasty little bird." Distracted and half bent over to try and grab the fleeing Benedict atop his oxen mount, Jingles never saw Charlie swoop low.

Santa leaped from the caribou's back, his swirling red and white sword extended, and, in a move that had everyone holding their breath, sliced neatly through Krampus' neck before gracefully alighting.

For a second, Jingles stood. Mouth open wide. Eyes even wider.

Thump.

Jingles' head hit the ground, and this time, the letting of blood didn't cause him to grow. The body did a slow slump to the ground and didn't move.

It took a moment before everyone realized the nightmare was over.

A mighty cheer arose that turned into a song.

"Jolly Old Saint Nicholas,
Aimed his sword this way!
Didn't spare this evil soul,
Or listened to what he said.
Christmas Eve is upon us now,
You dear and tough old man,
Give three cheers for Santa Claus.
He's our favorite man."

There was much rejoicing, and yet Nanook couldn't join them. He raced into Gingerbread Hall to find his girls gone, along with Anjij. Where were they?

Dancer skidded to a halt in front of him and quickly shifted to say, "We have to get to the factory, pronto."

Still a bear, he uttered a questioning, *"Grawr?"*

"The girls are in the candy-making factory with your ex-wife. Hurry. We have to stop her."

Stop Anjij from doing what? Surely Anjij wouldn't hurt them?

Dancer yelled the reply before racing for the factory, still billowing smoke. "She's trying to be the next Mastermind, and she's planning to start with your girls!"

With that shocking news, Nanook couldn't run fast enough.

Even then, he arrived to see he might be too late. A wall of animals crowded the factory floor, standing between him and his cubs. Perched on a catwalk above a massive vat, his girls stood on either side of Anjij, not by choice. She gripped each one by the hand.

"Let them go, Anjij," he shouted, keeping a wary eye on the sea of foes. They stared at him, the wolverines with drool dripping, the walrus, wobbling in place. Held in check for the moment.

A cruel tilt lifted the corners of Anjij's lips. "Why would I do that?" She laughed. "You're too late, Nanook. I've already won. Minions, attack!"

In that moment, he understood. It wasn't Krampus who'd been controlling the animals, but his ex. As the wild animals began throwing themselves in his direction, he couldn't help but feel regret that he'd failed. He'd never be able to save his girls with such terrible odds.

But even knowing that, he'd go down fighting.

With a mighty roar, Nanook raced to battle.

14

She was curvy and beautiful, a sexy polar bear,
And I felt slightly inadequate. I couldn't compare.
With a sneer to her lips and a toss of her hair,
Anjij let me know I was right to despair.
She spoke a few words, but I couldn't let her distract,
As Anjij ordered her army, I needed a plan of attack.
With more courage than I felt, desperation made me brave,
I scrambled for an answer and gave her a wave.

"Yoohoo, Mrs. Krampus," Dancer yodeled, loudly she should add, given the fight happening on the factory floor. When she'd entered and seen the waiting army, she'd immediately, and smartly, clambered up the nearest ladder to reach a catwalk that sat at a ninety-degree angle from the twins' mother. Although the term mother seemed misplaced in this situation. What kind of woman terrified her own children? Not that the girls looked that scared. More peeved. They glared at Anjij and had their expressions set in stubborn disapproval.

Seeing Dancer, Anjij's lips pursed. "How did you escape the yoke? All you doe-eyed idiots are supposed to be hauling the barrels so that they're ready for tonight."

"I don't work for despots," Dancer replied.

"Yet you toil for Santa," Anjij said with a sneer, having to practically shout to be heard over the snarling and thumping happening below them.

"Hardly a chore since Santa's always treated me right." Sure, he kept giving Rudolph first lead, but even she had to admit a shining bright nose to guide trumped her horns.

"I'm not surprised your oat-sized brain can't see how he's made you his slave and forced you to do his bidding."

"You mean like you forced poor Jingles to do yours?"

Anjij's chin lifted. "I didn't make him do anything. He was my partner."

"Partner?" Dancer snorted. "Everyone knows Jingles never had enough candy corn inside that head of his to ever imagine doing any of this." As Dancer spoke, she neared the other woman, her steps slow and measured. She didn't like how close Anjij had the girls standing to the edge of the catwalk and the vat below. While not steaming, the liquid would be deep enough to drown, not to mention, who knew what poison she'd dumped into it? What had she concocted? Dancer could see the aforementioned barrels ready to be loaded onto a wagon, her friends and coworkers, heads slumped, yoked, waiting for the order to pull.

"Jingles might have lacked the vision to grasp my plan, but he was involved every step of the way," Anjij declared.

"Did that include him agreeing to be turned into a monster?" Dancer reached the turn from her catwalk onto Anjij's.

"Neither of us knew what to expect when we came across Mastermind's recipe, but Jingles was excited. To go from diminutive and mocked by humans to fearsome was a dream of his."

"And you took it, too?" The very thought boggled the mind. Everyone knew Mastermind's concoction killed as many as it transformed. Even those who survived the experiment oftentimes suffered.

"Of course I tried it. All it took was a tiny drop to make me into the Queen of the North with everyone obeying my command."

"You control the animals," Dancer stated to clarify.

"It would seem the potion recognized my bodily superiority, hence why it unlocked the compulsion ability within me. Once I give an order, the simpleminded have no choice but to obey."

Dancer glanced at the chaos on the floor below caused by the animals under Anjij's control. Wolverines, walrus, and even a few birds were rabidly attacking, but not necessarily winning. While Nanook fought, he didn't do so alone. He'd been joined not just by their original party, but the elves as well. Everyone who could wield a weapon—or claw, or teeth—participated. Felicia the snow fox darted about nipping at hind legs. Gertie the musk ox head-butted, knocking down a walrus for the elves to pounce on with sharpened candy canes. Several polar bears slashed and snarled as they handled the frenzied wolverines. Even Leroy the snow goose dive-bombed the animals who couldn't stop themselves from attacking. Only Santa was missing. Probably dealing with the Yeti.

Thinking of him had her blurting out, "Why did you have Santa hooked up to that machine, draining his blood?" She'd been curious upon seeing it, but given the urgency of her task—eliminate Jingles—she'd not stayed to ask her unconscious boss.

"Isn't it obvious? I sought the reason behind his immortality. Everyone knows the man doesn't age."

"Looks pretty old to me," Dancer replied.

"And yet he's the same as he was ten years, ago, twenty, a hundred. Something stopped his biological clock, and I aim to find out what. Once I discover the secret to his longevity, I shall rule forever." Her declaration only lacked a villainous cackle.

"A simple blood sample wasn't enough? You were draining him dry."

Anjij shrugged. "But how much is enough? Better I take it all since keeping him prisoner would have been too dangerous. After all, he is a tricky fellow. Once I'd taken what I needed, the plan was, and still is, to eliminate him."

"Thereby depriving millions of children of the joy he brings every year."

A sneer tugged Anjij's lips. "As if I care about their feelings. And who says I won't have a surprise for the little beasts Christmas morning?"

The comment had Dancer glancing at the vat. "I assume this is the surprise?"

"Not just for the children. The liquid in there will bring about the dawning of a new age. Once those barrels are poured into the water reservoirs of the world, humanity will either change or perish. Either way, there will no longer be humans hunting our kind. No more hiding what we are. No more weak species. Predators shall rule the world."

The claim widened Dancer's eyes. "That's insane. You're talking about poisoning billions."

"Well, you know, climate activists do keep saying the Earth is overpopulated. I should think I'll be celebrated for solving that problem." Anjij, with her twisted mind, somehow managed to see herself as a heroine.

As the fight on the floor began to die down, the number of animals greatly diminished, Dancer kept Anjij talking as she inched closer. "Why did you steal the children from the encampment?"

"Because Jingles got overzealous. His orders were to grab my progeny, but then he decided, why not take all the children? Annoying things, keep whining they want their parents."

Wait, had Anjij been trying to save her cubs from her

devious plot? "You wanted to keep the twins safe from the poisoned water?"

"On the contrary," Anjij said with a laugh. "My daughters will be the first I transform that they might inspire others to join us."

"Over my dead body," an impressively naked Nanook roared. He stood in front of the vat, glowering.

Unlike Dancer, Anjij didn't appear impressed. "Dead is how I would prefer you, but like a gnat, you just can't stop pestering. So annoying. I'll be glad when I'm rid of you."

"Don't you hurt my Dada!" Siku huffed.

"Quiet. I didn't say you could speak," Anjij spat, her expression far from maternal.

"You're a mean lady," Sesi stated. "I don't like you."

"Is that any way to talk to your mother?" Anjij snapped, squeezing Sesi's arm. Rather than flinch, the child scowled.

"Already told you, not our mama," Siku stated stubbornly.

"I am, and you will obey me."

"No, I won't," Sesi exclaimed. "Want my Dada."

"Me too." Siku's lip jutted.

"You can't have him." Anjij got a look of concentration on her face, and the reason why smashed its way inside a moment later. The Yeti must have had their fill of fruitcake. Despite looking annoyed at being summoned, with their beards and mustaches shedding crumbs, they stomped their way toward Nanook, who not once looked over his shoulder. He kept his gaze on his ex.

Nanook crossed his arms and grimaced. "I'd say I regret marrying you, but the twins are the best thing to ever happen to me. You, however, should have stayed gone. This won't end well for you, Anjij."

"I never planned to return. However, I needed Santa's factory and his ability to deliver around the world. A world that needs a good smack. Sunbathe just once as a polar bear and people start screaming, followed by the guns coming out. So annoying. Once I realized I couldn't live as I wanted, in my furry skin, I knew I had to change how things were."

The Yeti were within grabbing distance of Nanook, and Sesi shrieked, "Dada, abomminy monster behind you!"

Despite the danger, Nanook didn't turn. He stared at his girls and Anjij intently. Conveying last words of love? Glaring deadly daggers at his ex? Why didn't he fight?

Unlike him, Dancer couldn't stand still. She bolted for Anjij, who controlled the Yeti. Kill her, stop the problem.

Anjij didn't look worried one bit. Then again, she only had to say, "Are you really going to murder me in front of my two innocent daughters?" for Dancer to halt in her tracks.

On the one hand, Dancer didn't want to traumatize the girls. On the other, if their dad died and mom got custody, they'd hate life even more. And that was only if they survived the splash into the vat their mom promised to deliver.

While she debated what to do, Nanook grunted as a

Yeti grabbed hold and lifted him, preparing to make him a polar snack.

Sesi glanced at Siku, and something passed between them. Something that had them both nodding, and to Dancer's astonishment, they whirled on Anjij and yelled, "Not our mama," before shoving Anjij into the vat with their tiny little hands!

15

> God rest ye grumpy polar bear,
> Who wished he'd done much more.
> He would have liked a last beer,
> Or a chance to even the score.

THIS WAS THE END. Eaten by a Yeti. Nanook could have transformed, but he'd only be delaying the inevitable, as the Yeti had him in a tight grip. Time to accept the fact that Anjij had won.

She'd fooled Santa.

Taken over the village.

Kidnapped his girls.

Now, threatened to destroy the world.

How someone so lacking in morality could have succeeded in her devious plot he didn't know, and his dumb ass had never once suspected the core of evil at the heart of her.

The depressing thoughts kept pushing as the Yeti lifted him toward its mouth. Without a fight, which was when it occurred to Nanook that he wasn't one to usually give up.

He'd not given up when he'd been in that jungle facing down that very angry hungry hippo. He'd not given up when he and that seal had gotten caught up in a fisherman's net. He'd come home with the seal and a slick yellow hat. When Anjij betrayed him, yes, he'd relocated, but he didn't stop living.

Entirely.

Okay, so he did sulk, but he still kept on going and was always there for his girls. Yet, for some reason, with Anjij's army lying in bloody pieces on the floor but for two Yeti, suddenly he was going to just let himself die?

It would be easier to just let it happen.

A thought that wasn't his.

"Get out of my head," he muttered. Asking didn't work. The pressure hammering at his free will increased. Even worse, he couldn't shift and fight.

He glared at Anjij, who had a strained expression but still smirked in triumph—until the twins pushed her off the catwalk and into the vat.

Splash.

The intense pummeling of his mind ceased abruptly, and suddenly, Nanook wasn't in the mood to get chewed on. He furred out, and the Yeti dropped him. However, when Nanook would have taken on the abominable beast, he found himself without an opponent. The Yeti neared the vat with interest, even as Dancer grabbed the girls and tugged them away from the view of the churning happening within the oversized container.

Anjij thrashed as she surfaced, spitting the fluid and blinking it from her lashes. "You wretched little mongrels," she screeched. "I'll...I'll..." Her voice deepened, and a growly rumble entered it. "What have you done?" she gargled as her large hands, the knuckles suddenly hairy, gripped the edge and she heaved herself over.

Anjij hit the floor with a splat, and no one approached. Everyone watched with bated breath as Anjij began to sprout fur. White fur, normal for a polar, only it grew shaggier than normal. Her body expanded, too, rending her clothes into rags, her breasts becoming pendulous and hairy, her hips wider. Her features also changed, getting thicker and more brutish. Horns peeked from her silvery gray hair. She pushed herself to her very large feet, which had burst out of her boots. "What is happening?" she asked in a low octave.

The Yeti closest to her sniffed and nudged his companion. They both leaned closer to inhale, before they both reached to touch. Anjij smacked one of the hairy hands and snapped, "Stand back, beast."

The one she'd hit hooted and thumped its chest. The other sighed and took a step back.

The Yeti she'd chastised then proceeded to grab Anjij, ignoring her failing fists and shouts. "Unhand me. I command you."

To which Santa, who'd just entered, replied, "I'm afraid Manchi won't ever let you go. You gave him the ritual mating smack."

"The what?" Anjij yelped.

"When you slapped Manchi, you signified your

choice of him over his brother, and now, he shall take you to his cave in the very far North, where you will have his children and tend his ice cave."

"No. No. I won't do it." Anjij screeched as Manchi tossed her over his burly shoulder.

"You will, or you'll die," Santa's quiet proclamation. "Your actions were grievous, but I'm willing to overlook them seeing as how you're the first female Yeti I've seen in decades. I'd feared poor Manchi and his brother would be the last of their kind, but now, with you, they have a chance to procreate."

"I'm not an abominable snowman," Anjij yelled as Manchi and his brother began marching for the hole they'd made in the factory wall.

"You are now, and it's your own fault," Santa said with a shake of his head and a tsk. "You should have never played with things you didn't fully understand."

"Help!" Anjij shrieked, to which the gathered elves began to sing, "Nah, nah, nah, nah, Nah, nah, nah, nah, hey, hey, hey, goodbye!"

It was oddly fitting.

Once the Yeti left, everyone kind of stared at each other before cheering. Not Nanook. He leapt onto the catwalk, kneeling so his girls could slam into him for a crushing polar bear hug. Which lasted two seconds before Sesi complained. "Dada, you need some clothes."

"Yeah, Dada. No one wants to see your junk," Siku sagely added.

Nanook closed his eyes and cursed his nephews

silently. "I will try and find something," he promised. "Are you girls okay?"

"Yes. We met elves," Siku declared. "The grown-ups are shorter than us!"

"We ate all kinds of candy," a bright-eyed Sesi exclaimed.

"And chocolate."

"We learned all about Santa Claus."

"And Christmas. You hid it from us," Sesi added with an admonishing note.

"Not anymore!" Siku shook her finger at him. "We want a tree."

"And presents. Lots of them."

"I'll do my best," his weak reply.

"I'll help," Dani murmured.

He glanced at Dani over his daughters' heads. "Thank you for trying to save my cubs."

"Don't thank me. I hesitated."

"Because you were thinking of my girls." He hugged them until they grumbled.

"Choking."

"Dying."

He released them, and they ran off in the direction of the big man who'd drawn a crowd, squealing, "Santa!"

How quickly they learned. How dumb he'd been to blame Christmas.

"Impressive fight. It was brave of you to try and take them all on by yourself," Dani said.

"Not as brave as you."

"We were all awesome!" Kira declared from below

the catwalk. "Catch!" She tossed him a blanket. "Wear this for now until I find something to fit your fat ass."

"It's not fat!" he huffed.

"If you say so," Kira sang as she headed back for her boys and husband, who stood clustered around Santa, along with the other children from FARTZ.

"Now what?" Dancer asked.

"Guess we find a place to stay for a few days while we figure out a way home."

"Oh." Her head ducked.

"Ahem, this is where you invite me to stay with you."

Her gaze met his, and her cheeks heated. "I mean, yes, of course you can. My cabin will be tight with the girls, but I'm sure we can—"

"Oh, the girls won't be sleeping with us." He shook his head. "Knowing them, they'll want to be where the action is."

He spoke of the yearly Christmas Eve overnight sleepover in Gingerbread Hall, where the elves dumped all their kids with the elders so that mom and dad could have a night to themselves to celebrate the year's hard work. It usually led to a bunch of elf babies being born around the same time. April was a busy month for birthdays. This year, however, given the destruction, it appeared they were setting up camp in the square given the number of braziers being lit and tents erected.

"I'd like that very much," she murmured.

"I'd say we both earned a kiss." He drew her up to his mouth and savored the sweet candy taste of her lips. Enjoyed even more how she sighed and melted against him. He was ready to toss her over his shoulder abominable-style and stomp off for some private time. However, they couldn't sneak off quite yet.

Amidst the rejoicing, the cleanup began. The elves sang as they went to work, forming a chain with wheelbarrows to remove the animal carcasses and wheel them to the butcher. The larders would be full and many new coats, boots, and muffs created from the remains.

Dancer went to speak with her reindeer friends, who emerged from the yoke looking exhausted and battered. Rudolph's nose wasn't just redder than usual. It had been broken and sat askew. More than a few limped.

While Nanook and the other polars handled the heavy lifting, he kept an eye on his girls, who chose to aid the elfin children in sweeping and moving the smaller pieces of debris into garbage bins. So much damage. Full-scale renovations and repairs would be needed for the hall, which might be why Santa sidled close to Nanook and cleared his throat.

"Lots of work to be done in the village," Santa muttered.

"Aye," Nanook replied.

"Could use some strong men to help."

"Yup."

"Well?" Santa eyed him, and Nanook sighed.

"I don't know if I can come back. Everyone knows why I left."

"They do, and honestly, no one ever spoke disparagingly of you. Anjij and Jingles' actions at the time shocked us all. So, I wouldn't worry on that score.

Besides, they've got better gossip now. Or haven't you been listening? All everyone can talk about is how you and the others bravely rushed in to save the day. You're a hero. You all are."

Hearing that coming from Santa's lips did much to puff Nanook's chest. "Just doing what was right."

"And that's why you've always been on my good list."

For some reason, the praise had him cringing. Nanook glanced at his bare feet. Cold but not horribly so, the floors in the hall being heated. "How can you still think I'm good when I turned my back on you and Christmas?"

"Because it's what's in your heart that matters."

Hearing the high-pitched giggle of Sesi, Nanook mumbled, "Guess my girls won't be too happy Christmas morning. I assume they're on the forever naughty list, given they shoved their mother in that vat."

"Punish them for doing the right thing? They could have done much worse and still been considered good girls."

"Thanks for not forgetting them." Nanook ahd grumbled each time he saw the unmarked packages for his girls, but he'd never destroyed the gifts.

"I kind of blame myself for what happened. I can't believe I didn't see the darkness in Anjij, both in the past and then again when she showed up on my doorstep," Santa grumbled.

"I don't think anyone ever knew just how much hate she harbored." Against the world. Nanook gestured to the vat. "What are you going to do with that poison she concocted?" The elves had cordoned off the area with caution tape that encompassed even the spills on the floor.

Santa's expression turned grim. "I'm going to need to dispose of it very carefully. Even a few drops in the water could have a dire effect on the ecosystem. Most likely I'll have to drain it into barrels and have them moved to a secure area for storage. I'll keep a small sample to experiment with to see if I can nullify its effect, though. Wouldn't want the wrong person to stumble across it."

"Could it really have changed humans into furries?" he asked.

"I'd rather we never found out." Santa slapped Nanook on the back. "Think about my offer. I really could use your help. Now if you'll excuse me, I need to see if we can still save Christmas."

The big man sauntered off, and Dani returned to his side. "Looked like an intense conversation. Everything okay?"

"Santa offered me a job."

"Oh." Nothing more than that one syllable, but it led to him glancing at Dani.

"A job would mean me sticking around the Village for a while."

Her lips curved. "I can't lie and say I'd hate that."

"Me either." He wanted to explore this burgeoning thing between him and Dani. "But I'll have to run it by my cubs."

"Understandable, although I don't think they'll

mind." Sesi and Siku were currently playing tag with the other children.

It tightened his throat. "I've deprived them of a normal childhood and friends."

"I wouldn't say deprived. They're young, and up until now, you were what they needed. A loving and involved father. But, yes, they're reaching an age where they'll want to explore more and develop friendships."

"Speaking of friends, how are all of the other reindeer?"

Dani grimaced. "Not doing so good. Anjij literally treated them like beasts of burden. She forced them to keep their reindeer shape, fed them nothing but oats and water, and abused them when they refused to obey. Rudolph got the brunt of it. Apparently, he didn't like not being in charge and kept arguing. He's got bruises all over, and his nose will likely never be the same again."

"Maybe he'll lose some of his arrogance," Nanook replied. He'd met the red-nosed hotshot a few times when here before and always had to curb an urge to give him shining black eyes.

"Doubtful. But I don't want to talk about him. I've got something much more important to handle right now."

"And what would that be?" he asked, hoping she'd drag him to her cabin to finish their kiss.

"Food. I am starving. All that shifting and running. This reindeer is starved."

So was he, as it turned out. A good thing the elves were already cooking up a feast. Trestle tables were set up in Holiday Square and a buffet filled them. A band began to play. Nanook got offered a sweet Adirondack, Santa-sized, so fit for a bear. With his belly full, and Dani in his lap, it wasn't long before they both ended up having a very cozy nap.

And woke to a hubbub.

People wailed, and when Dancer asked why, the elf closest to her pointed to the barn.

Dani took off at a run.

Despite wanting to sleep another twenty-four hours, Nanook followed.

16

O come all ye faithful, who freed Santa's
   Village,
Oh come, ye, oh come ye, to save
   Christmas Day.

AS DANCER ENTERED THE BARN, elves with woebegone expressions exited. She heard them murmuring and lamenting among each other. "Can't believe we have to cancel Christmas." "All that work for nothing." "The poor children."

Surely they exaggerated. Then again, maybe not. Anjij had shown a callous disregard for everyone, even her own kids.

Santa stood by his giant sled, the exterior sleek and a bright shiny red, its runners a glittery silver. A glance showed the top of the magical sack peeking from the back.

"Is there a problem with Big Red?" she asked,

noticing Santa's rounded shoulders and defeated expression.

"Sled's fine."

"Is it the presents?"

Santa shook his head. "The bag of toys is surprisingly intact. Anjij didn't bother dumping it and had only just started loading barrels into it. The elves removed them already." He waved to the barrels stacked against the wall.

"What's the problem, then? The elves are saying Christmas is cancelled."

"Can't deliver toys if there's no one to pull the sleigh."

"I'm ready and able," she corrected.

"But you can't drag it alone." Santa ran his hand over the smooth surface of the sled.

"The rest…"

"Are apparently in no condition to fly."

Dancer had to wonder about that. She'd been present when they'd been unyoked and tended by Dr. Longnose and her assistant, Nurse Redbottom. Their prognosis? A bit of rest and the reindeer would be fine. The problem being, today was the one day they needed to suck it up and push past their discomfort. However, reindeer could be prima donnas about their work conditions. They considered themselves in a different class from the elves and other workers in the village.

"Excuse me a second," she said to Santa, marching away from him and out the back to the cabins assigned to the team.

No need to knock on doors. The reindeer hung

around a cozy fire, wrapped in blankets, drinking spirits.

"What are you doing?" Dancer snapped. "Now is not the time to get drunk. We have a job to do."

"How can I work?" lamented Rudolph. "Have you seen my nose?" He waved to the crooked appendage.

"You don't need your nose to fly. The forecast is calling for clear skies."

"I'm too tired," whined Comet.

"Have you seen my leg?" Vixen had it propped on a stool, a small Band-Aid affixed to her calf.

Dancer's mouth opened and shut soundlessly before she burst. "Are you cotton candy kidding me? Santa needs us. The children of the world are counting on us."

"You heard the doc. We need rest." Rudolph slurred. "And liquid medicine." He sloshed his bottle of spiked eggnog.

"There will be 364 days to rest, starting tomorrow. We have a job to do."

"Can't."

"Sorry."

"Maybe next week."

The various excuses had Dancer seeing red. She whirled around and headed for the barn, almost slamming into Nanook in her ire.

"I take it your chat with your teammates didn't go well," Nanook stated.

"They're refusing to do the Christmas run. So what if they're a little tired and bruised? I am too. But I can power through it for one night."

DANCER AND THE ICE BEAR

"That's because you're made of tougher stuff than them," he remarked.

"Apparently. However, I can't pull the sled alone," she grumbled.

"Who says you'd have to? I have an idea." He whispered in her ear, and Dancer's eyes widened.

"Well?" he said.

"That might just work. Give me a second to run it by the boss." While Nanook headed around to the front, she trotted back into the barn, where Santa still eyed his sleigh with the saddest expression.

"Sir, it's getting late, You should be getting dressed," she advised.

"What's the point? Despite everything we've accomplished, Christmas is cancelled." Santa sighed. "Those poor children who've been good. I hate disappointing them.

Dancer cleared her throat. "Excuse me, sir, but I wouldn't be so hasty about pulling the plug quite yet."

"Did you convince the team to give it a go?" His expression turned hopeful.

"No. Even if I could have, they're much too sloshed. However, technically, we just need a replacement team to pull the sleigh."

Santa shook his head. "With who? We don't have enough reindeer, and while I've attempted in the past to do practise runs with the elves, they lack the size and strength to pull."

"There is another option. Come with me." She led Santa outside the barn and inclined her head to where Nanook stood chatting with Rook and Weaver. As she watched, the group was joined by Charlie, Kira, and Arnie. She pointed. "What if we harnessed five polar bears and a caribou?"

"They'd certainly be strong enough to make up for the lack of a full team," Santa mused aloud. "We could even adjust the harness to fit, and the flying dust will work on anyone. However, none of them know the route." Which was when he stared at her and said, "Dancer, with your mind so bright, would you guide my sleigh tonight?"

Dancer just about burst. "Hopping hollyberries! It would be an honor, sir."

A suddenly revived Santa beamed. "In that case, let's get this sleigh in the sky."

Things moved quickly after that. The elves, realizing they had a chance to save Christmas, pitched in to adjust the harness meant for reindeer to fit the bigger polar bears. They drew quite the crowd of watchers as they tethered the new team to the sleigh.

Before departing, Sesi and Siku hugged their father and only whined a little when they realized they, too, couldn't fly. However, they were soon distracted by the gingerbread that emerged fresh from the oven, running. A special Christmas treat, the shaped cookies liked to chirp at the kids, "Too slow. If you want to eat me, you'll have to catch me." The children hooted as they chased the cookies.

As the elves hooked Dancer to the front—first lead! —she did her best to not preen too much. Not easy, since this was a dream come true. She only hoped she

DANCER AND THE ICE BEAR

didn't mess up the route or the other reindeer would laugh and call her rude names.

Once ready, they stood at the end of the runway while Santa stood in the sleigh to give his yearly speech. "Dear friends, these past few days have been hard. Loved ones lost. Cherished things and homes destroyed. However, I am proud to be able to stand here and say we survived. Survived because of your indomitable spirit. Christmas is going to happen, and while I have to thank you all for your incredibly hard work, I think we owe an extra cheer for the group that came to our rescue and especially the reindeer who courageously set out to find that help. Let's hear it for the Polar Crew." The name he'd given the replacement team.

She liked it better than Rudy's Does.

"Hip, hip, hooray!" yelled the crowd.

Someone even sang, "Dancer, the sexy reindeer, had a very lovely rump. And when Nanook first saw it, he almost gave it a—" Someone stifled the singer.

Santa cleared his throat. "Thank you for that, Limerick. Now, if you don't mind, it's time we got going. Ready, Dancer?"

She bobbed her head, but before she could get going, a sloppy-drunk Rudolph came stumbling onto the runway, weaving and bobbing. "I'm here, Shhhanta," he slurred. "Dunna worry. I gunna guide da sleigh."

"You're wasted," Santa dryly replied. "Go home and sleep it off."

"But it's Krisss-mas. You need me," Rudolph stated as he started removing his clothes.

"What I need are people I can rely on, and they're already here, fit and ready for duty."

"She's in my spot." Rudolph fixed Dancer with a glare.

"Actually, she's earned first lead for her heroism in saving the Village and Christmas. Now, out of the way. I've got a present run to start."

A mulish expression on his face, Rudolph crossed his arms.

"I don't have time for this," Santa muttered.

"I got this, Santa," Gertie called out before stalking over to the red-nosed drunk. She grabbed Rudolph and heaved his complaining body over her shoulder before stalking off. Once more, the crowd cheered.

Santa cleared his throat. "It's time, team. Shall we?"

Heads bobbed, and a few bears sneezed as Santa flung the flying dust over them. Dancer inhaled deep, feeling the magic tingling as it entered her system.

"Polar Crew, move out," Santa ordered.

Bells jingled as they took their first step, everyone getting used to the harness and the fact they had to work together. They'd not had a chance to practice, so Dancer could only hope it would go well. The sled lurched. It took a few paces before the team found a rhythm and began to pick up speed.

Santa began to yell. "On Nanook, and Charlie, Arnie and Kira. On Weaver and Rook, and of course my lead, Dancer. To the end of the runway, then leap very tall. Now dash away, dash away. Dash away all."

There must have been something in Santa's terrible rhyme for they found a cadence and gathered momentum. Cool wind rushed past Dancer's muzzle and through her antlers.

Faster. She strained on her harness, a signal to the team to move their paws. When the world began to blur, she did a tiny leap and floated. They were ready. She let her hooves hit the ground and uttered a bleating cry before coiling her hind legs and pushing into the air.

For a second, those behind in the tethers almost yanked her down. But not for long, as everyone jumped, not gracefully or at the same time, but once they were in the air, it didn't matter.

They were flying, no friction, no obstacle, just how fast they could run.

As she led them, she heard the chuffs and huffs and even grunts of the excited bears at her back. Only Charlie remained sedate. After all, flying was in every reindeer's—and caribou's—blood.

"Take us to the South Pacific, Dancer," Santa hollered. "Let's deliver some presents."

For a team only formed that very same day, they did pretty cotton candy good. Sure, they didn't land neatly on all the roofs. However, the street worked just as good, especially since Leroy came along. He handled the chimneys they couldn't reach, gripping presents with his claws and slipping down into homes to drop them.

It took them all night to deliver everything—with a short delay at a home where some kits and cubs had stayed awake for a glimpse but were wrangled by their perky bunny mom—and dawn had started to lighten the sky as they dropped the last gift. They'd finished a little later than usual, but Christmas was saved.

However, their adrenaline and elation over that fact only lasted until they landed back in the North Pole. The dust Santa had used on them to give them stamina, speed, and more wore off and left them exhausted. More so than usual, given the days of stress Dancer had experienced. She fell asleep on her hooves as the elves removed the harness.

No surprise, she woke in her cabin with no idea how she got there, but she was quite happy to find Nanook lying under her.

Even happier when he rolled her under him and said, "Morning, Dani."

"Merry Christmas, Nookie," she replied.

"Is that a hint for your gift?"

Before she could lament she'd forgotten to get him anything, his lips touched hers, and she already knew it would be the best present ever.

17

> Joy to my world, he'll make me cum,
> Let my hearth receive his spear.
> Let my passion and eagerness receive his pleasure.
> And my pussy and heart will sing.
> And my pussy and heart will sing.
> And oh, oh, oh, oh, oh, my body screams.

DANCER ALMOST EMBARRASSED herself coming too fast. What could she say? Nookie's kisses melted her like a marshmallow over fire.

But she contained herself, kind of. His lips met hers, and she eagerly embraced him right back. Their breaths hotly shared between them. Their hands eagerly stroking and exploring.

They'd been put to bed wearing simple linen shifts, easily discarded that they might touch, flesh to flesh.

So much flesh for her to explore. Despite Nanook having rolled her under him, she shoved until she got him on his back. She straddled his wide body and let her hands skim across the muscled planes of his torso, exploring the ridges she'd been admiring. Tweaking his flat nipples. Drawing a gasp with everything she did.

"Dani." He moaned her name.

"What is it, Nookie?" she whispered against his neck as she nibbled the flesh that tempted.

"You're driving me wild."

"Good." Because he'd been doing the same since they met.

She kissed her way down his body, teasing the skin that shivered as he realized where she aimed for. His shaft stood tall and thick. A candy stick that she grabbed hold of, and, yes, she gave it a lick.

She wrapped her lips around the tip of him and sucked, tasted the pearl that decorated the tip, explored the length of him with her tongue. Revelled in how he groaned and bucked.

She would have gladly sucked and licked until she got a creamy surprise, but he growled and suddenly flipped her back onto her back, covering her body with his as he bestowed a fierce kiss.

Then it was his turn to explore, his mouth dragging sensation and heat everywhere it explored. Her nipples puckered, taut berries that he suckled. His big hands cupped her breasts and pushed them together that he might rub his bristly jaw, drawing a gasp at the sensation.

But she truly cried out when he slid between her legs and devoured her. He licked her until she bowed from the bed. Flicked her clit until she whimpered.

Only then did he slide back up her body until the tip of him nudged. She dragged him close for a kiss as he entered her, the thickness of his shaft stretching her so nicely. He grunted as she squeezed her muscles to hold him tight.

"You're making it hard for me," he murmured.

"So hard," she teased, wiggling her hips.

He stroked, in and out, thrusting evenly and deeply, perfectly. Her fingers dug into his broad back as he rode her, driving her pleasure up a hill and then pushing her off it.

She came with her mouth wide open, too breathless to cry out. Tense and yet boneless at the same time as she climaxed harder than she'd ever imagined. And to her delight, he joined her, shouting, "Dani!"

Then he collapsed.

On her, she should add.

But she didn't mind the weight of him. She hugged him tight and whispered, "My Christmas wish came true."

"Oh, and what did you wish for?" he mumbled against her neck where his face lay.

"To find someone who makes me happy."

He raised his head. His craggy features crinkled as he bestowed upon her the biggest smile. "Ditto. I used to think my life was fine, but then a reindeer crashed into my mountain and dragged me back into the world of the living, and people." He grimaced, but only for a second. "And you know what, I don't mind one bit. I'm glad we found each other. Although, I am sorry."

"Sorry for what?"

The door slammed open, as two little girls rushed in. "Told Gertie you were awake," Sesi exclaimed as Nanook slid off her and tugged up the blankets to cover them.

"She tried to say you were still sleeping, but I heard you yelling at Dani. Did she squish you in bed again?" Siku asked.

"Uh…" Poor Nanook turned bright red, so Dancer came to his rescue.

"I farted," she stated. "And it was so smelly."

"Mine are too. Auntie Kira says it's because we're stinking cute," Sesi stated as she clambered onto the bed.

"You slept for sooooo long." Siku climbed up on the other side.

"Did you have fun while I was working?" Nanook asked.

"Oh yes. We slept outside under the stars and watched a space movie. Next year for Christmas, I want a lightsaber," Sesi announced, bouncing up to pretend-swing her sword while making zinging sounds.

"I want to be Princess Leia," Siku exclaimed, not to be outdone.

"We got presents," squealed Sesi. "I got the prettiest doll."

"I got building blocks."

"We had pancakes with chocolate chips for breakfast and pizza for lunch." Sesi kept narrating their day.

"Santa gave Charlie a new helicopter, and he says he can take us home, but we don't wanna go," Suki stated with a jutting lower lip.

"I like it here, too. Do we have to go?" Sesi whined.

"What would you say if I told you Santa offered me a job?" Nanook drawled.

"So, we can stay?" Sesi cocked her head.

"Yes."

"Yay!" the girls squealed and bounced right out the door, yelling, "We gotta go tell our new friends."

He glanced at Dancer. "Guess that answers that question. I'm assuming you still want me around."

"Yes, although we might need a bigger bed."

And a lock on the door because more people chose to come barging in, thankfully after they'd managed to get some clothes on. Dancer had some in her dresser while a pile of folded garments had been left on a chair for Nanook.

Kira was next to enter without knocking. "The girls said you've decided to stay in the Village."

He nodded. "Santa offered me a job. Rebuilding and whatnot."

"Us too. He wants us all to relocate."

"Are you?"

"I'm thinking about it. It would be nice to have access to things without needing months for it to be delivered," Kira mused aloud.

"What about your house pods?" he asked.

Kira moved a hand. "They're moveable. I just need to stake out a spot for them." Kira headed for the door. "Speaking of which, I'd better choose a location before someone else gets the best view."

The entire Polar Crew came wandering in over that

next hour, each of them having been offered a chance to stay and all of them contemplating it, even Charlie.

"I'm not crazy about living around folks again," said the ornery caribou with a grimace. "But I was telling Santa some ideas I have for his sled, and now he wants me to work on a prototype with those elves. Guess it wouldn't hurt to stick around for a bit."

By the time Dancer and Nanook ventured forth, they discovered the elves had already started framing a building for their new residents to work out of, although Nanook did frown at the sign planted in front of it.

"BUTT?" he questioned aloud.

It was Ding-a-ling who proudly stated, "Welcome to the office for the Bispecies United Technical Team." Their new fancy title for non-elves employed by Santa's Village.

While Nanook discussed the details of the new build, Dancer wandered over to The Hot Cocoa and Donuts Shop in search of something to eat.

She ran into Rudolph, looking rumpled and bleary-eyed. She expected him to be mad she'd taken his spot, but instead, he slicked back his hair and offered a smarmy smile. "Today is your lucky day," he announced.

"Oh, why is that?" Dancer asked as she waited for her order of food.

"Because I've decided to take you as my mate."

"You have?" Her brow arched.

"It's only natural. First lead and second lead. We'll

make fine calves to take our spots when we get too old."

"No, thanks," she stated before taking a bite from a cream-filled donut.

"Er, what? You did hear me, right? I said I've decided to honor you by—"

She cut him off. "Not interested. I already have a mate."

Rudolph's brows rose. "You can't possibly mean that bear."

"That bear helped save this village and Christmas."

"But he's not a reindeer."

"And?"

"My nose glows."

She snorted. "So does a headlamp. Now if you'll excuse me, I've got a sardine donut to bring to the hero of Christmas."

With that, she left the shop with a bag and tray of drinks. Nanook took the treats from her and, in between bites, said, "Why's Rudolph keep scowling in our direction?"

She snorted. "Because I told him I wasn't interested in becoming his wife."

"He wants to steal you from me?" Nanook bristled and glared at Rudolph.

"Ha. I'd rather be single than date him. But no worries, Nookie. I told him, and I'll tell anyone else who asks, I've already got all the bear I need."

He swept her into his arms and swung her around before saying, "I still want to punch him."

"I know." And she just might let him.

After all, Nookie deserved a present for Christmas too.

EPILOGUE

We wish you a merry FUCmas,
We wish you a merry FUCmas,
We wish you a merry FUCmas and a
    happy BUTT year.

A YEAR LATER...

Much had changed since they'd saved Christmas.

Nanook officially relocated to Santa's Village, although not in Dancer's original cabin. He built a new home big enough for them and the girls.

"It's got five huge stalls!" she'd overheard a jealous Vixen say. Which, in normal terms, meant two bedrooms, a living room, kitchen, and indoor bathroom.

Kira ran the BUTT operation with an iron paw. Not only having the team help with the rebuilding of the destroyed hall, but also getting them to train just like the reindeer.

Rudolph had taken offense. "Santa has us! There's no need for a backup."

To which Kira, sweetly—if you ignored the teeth—replied, "Just in case someone gets a boo-boo again."

Santa made things slightly worse by telling Rudolph, "I haven't decided who's going to pull the sleigh, but I do know Dancer's my new lead. I want someone willing to risk it all for Christmas."

Yeah, she'd definitely moved up in the ranks just by doing the right thing, but the funny part? She no longer really wanted it. Sure, she accepted the position, but it wasn't as exciting as her new life with her bear.

Speaking of bears…

Turned out Santa's last run with his replacement team didn't go unnoticed. More than a few internet videos popped up showing the sled with its running polar bears. It led to new decorations being released later that year with, you guessed it, bears.

There was even a song that had Rudolph gnashing his teeth.

Nanook, the big butt polar,
has a very impressive growl,
And if you ever heard it,
You really shouldn't stick around.
Rudolph, the jealous reindeer,
Tried to laugh and call him names,
But stopped when Nanook's mate
Punched him in the kisser.

. . .

DANCER AND THE ICE BEAR

Yeah, it didn't really rhyme, but that didn't stop people from belting it out. And for those wondering, Dancer didn't mean to sock him in the nose. His face just happened to be where her fist landed.

Total accident. She was aiming for a fly, and if anyone asked, yes, she totally saw one.

Life was better than good with her mate and twin daughters, who decided early on to call her mama. She'd almost cried. She loved those cubs. Loved tucking them in, reading them stories, and just being their mom.

She also loved her hunky polar bear husband. Speaking of whom, she saw him sauntering toward their house, which led to the girls cheering. "Dada's home!"

Dancer let them race for him, never tiring of how his expression softened as he scooped them up and spun them around until they squealed. How had she ever thought him grumpy? With his family, he was the most loving man anyone could ask for.

As Nanook neared, his smile turned into that special one reserved for her. The smile that turned her legs to wobbly licorice.

"Hey, Dani," he murmured, drawing her close for a kiss.

"Hello, Nookie. How was your day?"

"Good. I had an interesting chat with Santa." He crouched to bring himself eye level with the twins. "Santa mentioned he didn't get a letter from you. I thought we were celebrating Christmas this year."

Sesi grinned. "We are. Did you forget we got a tree?"

"You helped us decorate it," Siku reminded.

"And we made cookies."

"Ooh, and then had to make more because Mama ate so many."

Dancer shrugged sheepishly. "The girls made my favorite. I couldn't resist."

"What about your letters, though? How's Santa supposed to know what to get you?" Nanook queried.

"We already got what we wanted," Sesi stated.

Siku nodded. "Yup, we did."

"Oh. And what was that?"

"A happy Dada."

"An awesome Mama."

And together they shouted, "And a baby brother!"

Dancer almost fell over laughing at his expression.

"Is it…Are you…" He was at a loss for words.

She nodded. "Yup. I'm preggers, so you'd better be ready because, in a few years, you'll be teaching junior to write his name in the snow with pee."

"Hot cinnamon sticks," he huffed. "We're having a baby!"

"Merry Christmas, Nookie."

It was much more than that. It was the happily ever after they both deserved.

NANOOK SPRANG TO THE ROOF AND GAVE A LOUD WHISTLE,
Friends and family came running, fast as a missile.
They heard him exclaim, 'I'm having a baby
Best FUCmas of all. I love my lady!'

. . .

DANCER AND THE ICE BEAR

Couldn't resist writing this FUC story when the idea hit. Hope you enjoyed it and Merry FUCmas to you. And remember, if you see a polar bear in the sky, be sure to wave hi.

Did you know I asked some author friends if they would like to write some stories based on my FUC world? As you can imagine, some of them had some interesting tales to tell. I do hope you'll check out the new FUC Academy books and giggle as you fall in love.

Looking for the entire F.U.C collection by Eve Langlais?

www.ingramcontent.com/pod-product-compliance
Lightning Source LLC
LaVergne TN
LVHW031540060526
838200LV00056B/4585